REPTILES

A feminist crime thriller

SYLVIA VETTA

Clapham Publishing Services

Cover and Interior Design by Petya Tsankova

ISBN paperback: 978-1-910461-90-7
ISBN ebook: 978-1-910461-91-4

Table of Contents

Dramatis Personae:
Main Characters

Thames Reach: A large village squeezed between the Thames and Bagley Wood and situated between Oxford and Abingdon.

THAMES REACH RESIDENTS

Alex Hornby: Crime writer. 51 year old Alex was the first non-white resident in the village.

George Gamble: Naturalist and photographer.

Sam Price: owner of the Studio Gym and 1 Abingdon way Air B&B.

Dr Yasmin Bell: gynaecologist and researcher into gene editing. Yasmin is the daughter of former diplomat, the historian, Professor Jonathan Bell.

& Iranian born lawyer and feminist activist, **Nazreen Bell**.

THAMES VALLEY POLICE

Detective Chief Inspector Ranjit Singh: Ranjit is of Sikh ancestry and formerly worked for the MET.

Detective Sergeant Kate Farr: Farr met and became friends with Alex Hornby during a previous case.

Detective Inspector Peter Jordan, Detective Inspector Veronica Chen and civilian IT expert **Richard Smith** complete the team.

THE JOHN RADCLIFFE HOSPITAL AND ASSOCIATED LABORATORY

Mr Darcy Moss: Consultant in Gynaecology and Obstetrics.

Dr Jim Azad: Research colleague working in Gene Editing.

Nurse Barbara Covet.

AMERICAN VISITORS

Serena Shriver: an influential Republican Christian Nationalist whose son,

Gideon, is working on a D Phil in Theology at Richmond College, Oxford.

Professor Steve Darwin: well-known and respected academic and wit; palaeontologist and expert on evolution.

OTHER

Geoff Hurst: journalist with the Daily Post

Dorothy Mead and **Thomas Said**: MI6 agents.

Foreword

My novels published by Claret Press are inspired by 'ignored history': important but often deliberately forgotten events. I wanted to write a book set where I live in the village of Kennington, only 1.5 miles from Carfax at the heart of Oxford but which is often ignored and underestimated. For the purposes of fiction, in *Current of Death,* I renamed it as Thames Reach. This sequel, set in 2025, given the state of the world, is darker and internationally connected. In all my fiction, I feel the need for a sprinkling of humour and hope.

Sylvia Vetta: May 2025

Chapter 1

'Born to spawn in the waters of their birth, the toads are drawn like magnets towards the lake.'
Alex Hornby

Alex was an optimist even if a realistic one. That was why she was struggling to be nonchalant about the email from Cheetah who made films for Channel 4. They wanted to talk to her about *Bad Blood in Summertown.* Her head was spinning, despite her intention to be calm and collected about it.

She'd drafted the synopsis of her next book and was setting the scene. The working title of *'A Novel Way of Death'* was inspired by a real case. The murder of local builder, Godfrey Price had appalled Thames Reach where she lived. Although large for a village, Thames Reach was accustomed to being ignored and was not dissatisfied with anonymity. The residents were happy to leave fame and drama to their near neighbours, the world renowned city of Oxford and Abingdon, the oldest inhabited town in the country.

Two suspicious deaths in close succession had catapulted the village into the national news. Ranjit Singh had just been appointed Chief Inspector in Oxford and it was his first case in charge of a murder investigation. His sergeant, Kate Farr and Alex had connected and quickly became friends. The murderer's confessional letter was addressed to the crime writer. Alex was planning to make use of that experience in her latest whodunit.

Wanting to give her aching eyes a break, she shut her computer and headed for 1 Abingdon Way, the home of Godfrey's young widow, Sam, short for Samantha. She'd been left pregnant and in financial difficulties. Alex and her physiotherapist neighbour, Cleo, had helped Sam kick start a new life. The large house, once known as the FORTRESS, had been transformed, divided into two dwellings and a fitness business with a welcoming aura. Samantha and Goldie, her now two year-old son, lived in the annex and the main house was let mostly on Air B&B. The gym, conservatory and swimming pool were used for Sam's new fitness enterprise. Business had been slow at first, but they were now being recommended by satisfied clients and membership was growing. Alex had joined and was more energetic because of it.

Sam gave her a warm hug and suggested coffee. They sat in the conservatory overlooking the garden. Her late husband disliked gardening and had paved over most of it. Wildlife friendly gardener, George Gamble, had volunteered to green it. At first, in Samantha's eyes, it looked untidy but nature was working its magic. She was surprised and delighted by bursts of life as flowers and blossom bloomed and enriched her life and the view from the gym offered nature's free gifts. The snow drops were out and the daffodils and crocuses starting to join them.

'I love snowdrops' said Alex. 'They are such hopeful little bulbs – augurs of spring - a bonanza of joy.'

There was a knock on the conservatory door. George leant on his rake and waved. Sam invited him in for a coffee but he pointed to his muddy boots saying.

'Thanks but no thanks. I'll come again at the beginning of March and do some tidying up but not too much, Sam. We'll talk about what bee and butterfly-loving plants to sow.' George saw Alex and beckoned her.

'Are you on for Toad Patrol? If the weather is mild and wet, they should start moving in a week's time.'

'Are you going to set up the doodle poll like last year?
He nodded.

'Email me, George, and I promise to sign up.'

City girl, Alex, was amused when she first heard about Toad Patrol after buying a house in Thames Reach. She witnessed residents wearing high-viz jackets patrolling alongside the old Abingdon Road during mating season to protect a throng of frisky toads, newts and frogs from being flattened as they bounced out of Bagley Wood to the pond near Chandlings School. George had explained it to her,

'Amphibians are not good at dodging traffic so we use torches to spot them as they near the kerb.' Alex joined the team twice a week the previous year. She learned to place the rescued in buckets. George identified them including their sex, recorded the numbers and carried the buckets across the road where they were released to finish their journey to spawn in their favourite pond.

'How many did we save last year George?' asked Alex.

'Almost 3,000...'

* * *

Just as Sam was pouring the coffee, a new client was about to leave after her swim.

'Can I introduce you?' asked Sam. 'This is my friend Alex Hornby - she's famous. Alex, this is Yasmin Bell.'

Alex blushed, not that Yasmin noticed: Alex's dark brown skin glowed.

'I suppose I am reasonably well known in Oxfordshire but I'm not a celebrity and I'd not want to be one. I prefer a quiet life in Thames Reach,' said Alex holding out a hand,

'Nice to meet you, Yasmin. Do you live in the village?'

'I moved here last year - to Woodland Road.'

'Oh, what number? I live at the Oxford end and I can't say that I've seen you before.'

'I live nearer the Abingdon end.'

'Where did you live before?'

'Boars Hill. My parents bought a house there when my father got an academic post so I spent my teenage years near here. And moved back in when I started at the John Radcliffe. When I blew out thirty candles, I was embarrassed about still living with mum and dad. Given Oxford prices, instead of a tiny flat I've a three bed semi with a conservatory and a small garden in Thames Reach. What a difference half a mile makes! I'm feeling lucky.'

'That's exactly why I moved here. Did you say your surname is Bell? Your father doesn't happen to be the historian? I was told Jonathan Bell lived on Boars Hill.'

'Yes, he's my father,' said a surprised Yasmin.

'Did you follow in your father's footsteps? Are you a historian?' asked Alex hopefully. Historians could be useful when it came to researching for writing.

'No way! I'm a gynaecologist but I take after him in one respect – I enjoy research more than clinical work. Sorry, I have to go – a twelve hour shift at the JR awaits me.'

***

Alex noticed that the main house was unoccupied.

'Have you any Air B&B's lined up, Sam?'

'Better than that, an American academic has booked it for six months - he's coming on sabbatical.'

'Where's he from and do you know his subject?'

Alex wondered if yet another geologist was attracted to Thames Reach. Sam looked in her diary.

His name is Steve Darwin and he's from Harvard - a philosopher and palaeontologist. He's coming alone at first but his son and family will join him at Easter.'

'Did you say Steve Darwin? The Steve Darwin who played himself on the Simpsons?'

Sam looked mortified.

'I wish I was well educated like you, Alex. Please tell me more about him. I don't want to embarrass myself when he's here – oh gosh, look at the time. I'm sorry, I have to dash. Goldie started at the Montessori last week – three mornings a week to begin with. Just let yourself out. Cleo's teaching Pilates but the session ends in ten minutes if you want to have a chat with her.'

Chapter 2

Two weeks later, at 7 pm on the last day of February, Alex donned her high vis jacket emblazoned with a quirky pic of a toad. Equipped with a torch and a bucket, she drove to the Old Abingdon Road and parked in the layby not far from Chandlings Manor Prep School. George and two other volunteers were already patrolling the verge. She signed in and George pointed towards an area of the road bordering Bagley Wood not yet covered.

She noticed there were already four toads and a frog in the large yellow bucket. It was ten minutes before she picked up her first moist frog which was just about to leap onto the road. The previous year, the act of picking up her first toad had been tinged with revulsion. Anticipating slime, she was surprised when the toad felt dry. After almost two hours and saving only three amphibians, she decided to call it a day. George made a suggestion.

'Traffic has quietened down now and not so many are coming so we can all finish. Would you like to come to the lake? We might as well take them all the way. There'll be a lot of activity. Fancy taking a look? See why we do this?'

'That sounds fun. Why not?'

They waved goodbye to the other volunteers and headed for the footpath. A few minutes later they reached the lake to be greeted by croaking in the reeds. It was the perfect time of night for mating. She watched as a smaller male climbed on the back of larger female. Then an almighty competition broke out as three other males tried to oust him. Alex found herself wondering whether there are certain times when human beings are more likely to feel frisky.

They unloaded their precious cargo and watched as they dived into the water. Alex took a slow walk around the lake and then climbed on to the wooden bridge to look down at active toads doing the breast stroke. Her eyes followed a female as she headed towards the bank. Poking out from the reeds she saw what looked like black plastic ... dangerous for wildlife. Alex climbed down the bank and stretched out her arm to pull it in. She screamed and George came running.

This could NOT be happening... no way does this happen more than once in anyone's life. Alex closed her eyes and said to herself,

'I'm imagining it.'

But she wasn't - George was on the phone to the police.

Lights flashed as three police vehicles drove into the school car park at speed. First on the scene was Detective Sergeant Kate Farr with a heavily built PC alongside her. Alex couldn't help it. She ran towards her and threw herself into Kate's arms. The male PC was none too pleased.

Kate's auburn hair was so tightly tied back that it looked painful and severe but she turned to her colleague and said,

'My friend is distressed, Constable Jones.'

She then took control of the situation. The recently promoted Inspector Chen joined her with two other constables. After talking photographs, she asked the PCs to drag the body onto the grassy bank ready for the forensics team.

The corpse had been floating face down in shallow water. They turned the body over. A look of horror spread across Kate's face. Although she was standing twenty yards away, Alex still had her torch in her hand and couldn't help seeing what Kate saw. The victim had been strangled.

Kate knelt down beside the body and with her gloved hard touched the end of the rope. Alex saw her recoil.

Kate called Veronica Chen to take a look.

They nodded at each other.

Kate said,

'That isn't rope or any man-made fibre. Do you think it is what I think it is?'

When their boss DCI Singh arrived with the forensic pathologist, it was confirmed that the victim appeared to be strangled by an umbilical cord. When they cut the thick black plastic covering the lower half of the body they were confronted with a hole where her womb had been.

Alex turned away and vomited. When she recovered she said,

'Kate, I know her. I met her at Sam's only two weeks ago. I met her: she was delightful. She's a doctor - Yasmin Bell- a gynaecologist at the JR. Who'd want to do that to her?' Kate asked the policeman to take Alex and George to the car.

'I'm sorry Alex but you know what I have to do. Once we've finished here, I'll come to the station and take your and George's statement. I wish it was possible to un-see what we've just seen.'

Chapter 3

At the station, Detective Sergeant Kate Farr struggled to control her emotions. She went to the bathroom, splashed her face with cold water, took a deep breath and made her professional training click in.

Before taking Alex's statement, she adopted a soothing low key voice.

'All we can offer is a strong cup of tea. You look as if you're in shock, Alex and between you and me, so am I. I've seen lots of things in this job that I'll never be able to forget but that was the stuff of nightmares.'

'Yes - a character finding a body in water more than once happens in my books but not in real life. For God's sake, this is Thames Reach! Until two years ago there was only one recorded murder in the entire history of the village. Now two years apart and two bodies both found by me and both known to me. What kind of weird coincidence is that? I came here to write 'cosy' crime but I've attracted a depravity that I can't cope with,' said Alex.

'Let's get your statements written down and then you and George can go home. Because I know you well, I'll get Peter Jordan to do it. Have you got a sleeping pill at home? Do take one.'

'I left my car on the Old Abingdon Road and George's bike is there. I'm not in a fit state to drive so I'll appreciate a lift.'

The previous year Kate Farr had bought a flat barely a hundred yards from Alex's house so didn't have far to go after dropping off Alex.

***

Alex woke wanting to scream but nothing came out. She remembered tossing and turning, unable to get the image of Yasmin out of her head but, looking at the time on her phone, she knew the pill had worked. She didn't *feel* hungry but once she started to have some breakfast, she knew she was hungry. Alex had not regretted becoming a full time writer until this moment. Going out somewhere to work would have helped today. How could she settle down to write after what she'd seen?

'I'm a selfish bit of shit. That poor family and what about Sam? How do I tell her that her latest client's been murdered? It's best if she doesn't find out in the papers.'

The author picked up a pen and clicked away at a rate more annoying than her usually tic. Before they left the police station, the Chief Inspector insisted she and George must tell no one about the presumed method of death or the mutilations to the body but it was acceptable to mention where the body was found.

***

Little Goldie came running to greet her...

'Auntie Alex, come, see.'

Alex followed the excited little boy to the conservatory. There in a basket curled up and asleep was a black and white kitten.

'Goldie, he's lovely.'

'No name. I like Spot.'

Sam came in smiling. She loved it when her son was happy.

'That's a good name. What do you think of the latest addition to our family, Alex? Kevin's cat had kittens. They were under the impression it was a boy so it came as a surprise.'

Kevin was Godfrey Price's son by his first marriage to Carol. At first he'd despised Sam but, after all they had been through, once Goldie was born, they tried to be more like a supportive family and Kevin tried to behave as an uncle to him. It helped that his mother Carol had forgiven Sam.

'When Goldie saw them, I knew he had to have one and Carol is having the other: keeping them in the family.'

The kitten woke and started to play with the soft ball by his bed. Goldie looked at Sam and she nodded.

'Yes, you can stoke him but very gently.'

Sam knelt down, picked up the kitten, placed him on a cushion and put the cushion on her lap. Goldie, trying hard not to grab at his fur, began to stroke him as gently as is possible. Only two, he was still learning to control his grip.

'Well done, Goldie. It's not easy to stroke gently. How about you tickle him but lightly with just two fingers?' Sam showed him how. The kitten began to purr and Goldie laughed.

Sam turned to Alex.

'You didn't come to see the kitten.'

Alex wasn't sure she could do this. How could she tell Sam especially with Goldie there?

'Sam I saw something distressing last night and want to forget it. Can I book in for a yoga session?'

'Cleo is giving one at two this afternoon. Come back then.'

Alex left without telling her.

***

At the station, Kate's boss, Detective Chief Inspector Ranjit Singh, assembled his team. Since the case of Godfrey Price, he'd led investigations into three murders. One was a 'domestic'- an angry man had killed his partner and then tried to kill himself. The second was a death by stabbing near Osney Wharf. That had been harder but once the victim was identified with the help of the public, it was clear that he'd been selling drugs and his death was gang related. The gang responsible was soon identified but piecing together the evidence to convict the perpetrator had been tricky.

The third murder case had been more distressing. Twenty-one year old Shabina Hussein was in her wedding dress ready to marry the man she loved when two of her cousins stabbed her twenty times. Her family had not approved her choice of husband. Ranjit remembered how Kate hated the way he had labelled it 'Honour Killing.' It was the most 'dishonourable' thing she could imagine.

The importance of team work was now ingrained in Ranjit's thinking. He knew he had to make an effort to show Detective Sergeant Farr that he appreciated her. He'd been guilty of undermining her in a jokey manner, during their first case together. During the Hussein case, she'd accused him of male bias. After that disagreement, he tried to change by challenging himself. Ranjit's children, Roshan and Amber were keen football players and Ranjit decided that his method should be that of a good coach encouraging whoever was in the best place to score. He looked at Chen, Jordan and Farr and felt confident.

Some pictures of Dr Yasmin Bell were on the board. In one, she was giving a lecture. Photos of her parents were on either side of her portrait pic.

'Professor Jonathan Bell is a well-known historian; his research topic is Middle Eastern history. His wife, Nasreen, was born in Iran when it was ruled by the Shah. She was nineteen when the Ayatollahs took over and her wardrobe had to change from bright colours to black and her flowing hair hidden under a tight fitting hijab. Nasreen and Jonathan met when he was working in the Diplomatic Service and was based in Iran. Their marriage probably saved her life.

'She'd become a feminist lawyer and active opponent of the regime's laws on female dress code. Rumour had it that the Revolutionary Guard were going to arrest her. Jonathan and Nasreen hastily left the country in 1989 using his diplomatic privilege. She retrained in British law and works as an immigration lawyer. She is 62, ten years younger than her husband. They never returned to Iran and when Jonathan left the diplomatic service, he took up a post at Worcester College in nearby Oxford. They bought a house in Boars Hill.'

'Has anyone told her parents?' asked Kate.

'I'm heading for Boars Hill as soon as this meeting ends. Come with me.'

'Are you going to tell them what was done to her?'

'No, not yet: I can't stress enough how important it is that the details do not leave this room. If we are going to catch whoever did this, this knowledge could be the key to provide the evidence to convict him or her.'

Kate felt certain that this was male violence but she tried to drive the thought from her head. She needed to be professional and not approach this case with preconceived ideas.

Chapter 4

Beechlands was, as the name suggested, surrounded by beech hedges. Ranjit rang the bell next to the tall gates. They opened slowly and Kate drove in. The blue door was opened by a distinguished looking man. He didn't look 72. He had a straight back, a flat stomach and his large brown eyes looked directly at Ranjit.

'Come in. To what do I owe the honour of this visit?'

'Is Mrs Bell in?'

'No, she's doing a stint volunteering at Asylum Welcome.'

'Sir, please can we sit down. I regret that we are bearers of bad news.'

The smile left Jonathan Bell's face as he ushered them into the lounge.

'I am so sorry, sir, but the news concerns your daughter, Yasmin Bell. We were called out to Chandlings Manor School last night. A body was found in the lake and we have reason to believe that it is your daughter.'

Jonathan put his hands over his face and appeared to choke. A trembling hand took out his mobile phone and rang a number, presumably Yasmin's but there was no ring tone. He made a conscious effort to speak carefully.

'Yasmin likes to keep herself fit and does sometimes go running in Bagley Wood but I can't believe she would run there in the dark. There must be some mistake.'

'There is no easy way of saying this, Sir. It was not an accident. Your daughter was murdered.'

Kate watched as the diplomat, used to controlling his emotions, break down. He clenched his fists and took a deep breath and spoke slowly and deliberately.

'How can you be sure it is Yasmin?'

In as quiet a tone of voice as he could manage, Ranjit replied,

'The body was found by Alex Hornby who recognised her. Once she gave us Yasmin's name, we were able to access pictures of her on the internet. It's the worst thing to ask of a parent, but we will need you to do a formal identification.'

'What business had that woman there after dark?'

'She's from Thames Reach where your daughter ...'

Ranjit was about to say 'lives' but corrected himself...

'lived. Alex was a volunteer on Toad Patrol. Living here on Boars Hill you've probably seen them in high-vis jackets on the Old Abingdon Road. Two of them had carried buckets of rescued toads to the lake.'

He didn't look convinced but asked,

'How was she killed?'

'She appears to have been strangled, sir. We are waiting on the pathologist's report to confirm it.'

'Who would want to do that to Yasmin? She only ever helped people. Hornby must have made a mistake. It can't be her.'

He looked stricken as if starting to believe it but wanting to deny it.

'We have to ask you to identify the body. I promise you that we will be unstinting in our efforts to find the person who did this to your daughter.'

'Is there someone who can be with you?' asked Kate.

'I do... don't know how I'm going to tell Naz. Yasmin is - *a quiet sob* - our only child.'

'Would you mind telling us when you last saw Yasmin?'

'Sunday. When she isn't working, she comes here most Sundays.'

'We'll appoint a liaison officer who will keep you informed about our investigations and help in any way she can.'

'I need to call Nasreen. When will you want us to ...'

'We'll send a car for you late tomorrow and afterwards, we would like to talk to you about your daughter. Is there someone who can stay with you?'

'I want to be alone when Nasreen comes home.'

With that they made their exit, leaving him to his grief.

***

Alex arrived ostensibly for her yoga session. Goldie was having an afternoon nap, so she knew that it had to be now or never. Alex suspected that, once the police had informed Yasmin's parents, they would release the news to the local press.

'Sam, I've something I need to tell you. Can we sit?

'After your session: Cleo's about to start. The others are already here.'

'I'm sorry Sam. Yoga was an excuse. Don't worry I'll pay for the session. Goldie was so excited this morning that I couldn't spoil the moment.'

Sam looked stressed and said,

'Let's go into the kitchen.'

They sat facing each other.

'You know that George and I volunteer on Toad Patrol.' Sam nodded.

'Last night we carried the amphibians all the way to the lake with the intention of stopping to watch some of them mate.'

'I don't know how to tell you. I don't want to believe it happened but what I saw is etched into my brain. I discovered the body of a client of yours, Yasmin Bell. She'd been murdered, Sam. It wasn't an accidental drowning.'

Sam began to shake. Alex got up and hugged her.

'You've only just begun to recover from Godfrey's death.

Because you know Yasmin, I didn't want you hearing or reading the news tomorrow. Social media is already speculating about the police activity at Chandlings.'

'I'm so very sorry for YOU, Alex. You found Godfrey and now Yasmin...'

'It feels like something out of a Greek Tragedy – as if I'm doomed. I don't want to believe it Sam, but I can't get the image of her out of my mind.' Alex's hands covered her eyes and tears began to darken the colour of her white scarf.

'Who on earth would want to do that? Her career is helping people,' asked Sam. Alex looked at her through tear-filled eyes and shrugged her shoulders.

'Our business has only just started to be profitable. That sounds so selfish but to be linked to three deaths...'

'I can't imagine that her death is associated with the Studio Gym and Frank's death was an accident so I don't think you need worry about that.'

They were referring to the death of Alex's neighbour, Councillor Frank Foreman, not long after the death of Sam's husband. Foul play had been suspected but it turned out to be an accidental death. Sam made tea for them both and they drank in silence until they heard the yoga session finish.

'We have to tell Cleo.'

***

On Boars Hill, Nasreen Bell let out a primal scream.

Chapter 5

Ranjit's parents had, like many Asian immigrants, wanted him to train as a doctor. Watching his first post mortem, he knew he'd made the right decision not to go into medicine. He observed the forensic pathologists and how they were respectful but detached in what they did, otherwise they couldn't do it. As Ranjit headed for the lab, he attempted to get into a similar mind-set, knowing that he was likely to fail miserably.

An hour later, he headed for his car feeling almost too sick to drive. He sat for a while thinking about what he now knew. The time of death 2-3 pm and the place of death probably not where the body was found. She had died of suffocation and the cord was used as some bizarre decoration. Because the body was in water, most evidence related to the 'where' was gone, but a surgical scalpel had been used to desecrate the body. Dominic Frankum would make sure the body was presentable for Yasmin's parents to see through the window. He would only reveal the head and shoulders. Kate Farr had been assigned the distressing task of accompanying her parents. How could they ever tell them that she may have been alive when her womb had been removed? The use of the umbilical cord to appear to strangle her surely indicated a hospital somewhere in the chain of events. Yasmin worked at the JR. That is probably where they should start their investigations.

***

Detective Chief Inspector Ranjit Singh summoned his team. He began by summarising what they knew.

'Thirty-three year old Dr Yasmin Bell grew up in the area, living with her parents until she moved to Woodland Road in Thames Reach eighteen months ago. She'd recently been promoted to senior registrar at the John Radcliffe Hospital doing three twelve-hour shifts per week. In addition to that, she was involved in some research projects. Chen, you look into her clinical work and Kate, take a look at the research projects.'

'The source of the umbilical cord is crucial but how do we investigate that without revealing why we need to know?"

No one answered.

'Come on, I need help here. Ideas please, even if they seem outlandish.'

Chen was the first to answer.

'When we are looking into her practice and the running of the department and research, we could just appear curious and get some info that way?'

'Good start... anymore?"

'Could we have a constable go to hospital ostensibly investigating another case, the dumping of hospital waste at a waste disposal site?' suggested Jordan.

'Good idea, DI Jordan. Who do you suggest we send? Chen and Kate, I can trust you to follow up a remark without raising suspicion.

'Let's consider other lines of enquiry. Alex Hornby, finder of bodies, says she met Yasmin at Thames Reach Studio Gym. Kate, can you follow that up? Find out how often she went there, when last she attended and if they know of any friendships. The parents told us that she was seeing someone when she moved to Thames Reach - a fellow researcher - but they sensed they'd had a row.'

Ranjit looked thoughtful. Heavy seconds passed before he continued.

'Here's the tough question. The method of her death doesn't look to me that it was a murder committed in a moment of rage. It had to be premeditated. It may be useful to call in a forensic psychologist to give us an idea of what sort of warped mind committed this. What do you think - any suggestions?'

Ranjit felt a twitch of disappointment when no-one replied. It was Kate who broke the silence.

'Have you heard of Serena Shriver of the Republican National Coalition for Life (RNCL), supporter of Operation Save America? Her son Gideon is studying theology at Oxford. She led an intimidating US style demonstration against abortion at the JR only a month ago. The 'Bodies, Rights, Power' group of feminists turned up to support the nurses and doctors including Yasmin, who worked there. The clash was reported in *The Oxford Times*, so I looked up what the group was saying about it. One of her colleagues said Gideon was shouting the name of Yasmin Bell accusing her of 'playing God'. It could be worthwhile if Richard delves into social media around that time.'

The team were impressed. Ranjit didn't quite manage to express his admiration but just said,

'Thank you Kate. That's a lead for your investigation at the lab. It's time to let the media have a statement and ask for anyone with information to call us.'

The local media had been touch and Ranjit had promised them a Press Release. He set about drafting one and took it to the Chief Constable to edit and distribute.

***

Kate decided she'd make the visit to Sam before the trickier enquiries at the hospital. Sam was not surprised to see her walking up the drive. She opened the door and said,

'I've been expecting you. Alex came yesterday. I've never seen her so upset. She'd only met Yasmin once but it must have been the shock of finding another body.'

Kate could guess the reason but wasn't going to tell Sam. They were about to sit down in the conservatory, when a well-built man carrying a towel walked in.

'Sorry to interrupt Sam. You said it's okay for me to use the pool.'

'Oh, this is Professor Steve Darwin, Kate. He moved in today.'

'And very nice it is and I appreciate the warm welcome,' said Steve Darwin holding out a hand.

'Kate lives in the village, in Woodland Road,' said Sam, hoping that Kate would not tell him the reason for her visit.

'You'll find it's a friendly village as long as you make a little effort to join in. And of course, it's so convenient. What brings you here, professor? asked Kate.

Professor Darwin looked thoughtfully at Kate as if analysing her before replying.

'I received an interesting email from a medic who lives in Thames Reach. I met her at a conference last year. She emailed me concerning her research. Something was bugging her. I was due a sabbatical. I thought I could kill two birds with one stone, as you Brits say. I wanted to catch up with an old colleague, Dr Gavin McGeorge who works at the Natural History Museum.'

Kate looked interested so Steve continued,

'Do you know him? 'Bugging' isn't probably the right word, disturbing is better. I guess the word 'bug' came into my head because my friend Gavin is jokingly called Dr Bug. We've published papers together. We are organising a workshop and I thought I could also help Dr Bell discover who is harassing her and hindering her research.'

'Did you say Dr Bell? That wouldn't by any chance be Dr Yasmin Bell?'

'Why yes. Do you know her?'

'Professor Darwin, would you mind joining us, please,' said Kate ushering them to sit down. Kate confessed,

'I am a friend of Sam's. That is true. But today, I'm here on police business. In the line of duty I'm known as Detective Sergeant Farr. I've a pressing reason to know more about your correspondence with Dr Yasmin Bell. I'm sorry to inform you but you won't be meeting her. I hope you haven't had a wasted journey. The fact is her body was found not far from here. She'd been murdered.'

Chapter 6

Kate rang Ranjit with the news,

'We've had a surprising break-though, Sir.'

She described her encounter with Professor Darwin.

'He's willing to send us copies of their correspondence and help in any way he can. The last time Sam saw Yasmin was the day she introduced her to Alex - not much use there but she was able to fill in a little about Yasmin's private life.'

'Go on. Don't keep us waiting,' said Ranjit.

'She had a relationship with another doctor at the JR. Sam doesn't know his surname but Yasmin called him 'Jim'. Because they were both registrars, they didn't have much spare time but they tried to meet over a meal at least twice a week. Sam assumed that it was about more than an interest in food...

'She said that Yasmin looked upset one day, in early December, when she arrived at the gym. The Studio Gym is a small business and Sam's interested in people so her clients often confide in her. Sam was confused by it because she didn't think the break-up was anything to do with their personal life. She mentioned a consultant called Moss – something about being 'a danger to women'. The trail seems to be leading us to her work, Sir. What do you think? '

'You and Chen need to get to the JR right now!' insisted Ranjit.

****

'Shit ... sorry for the language.'

Parents were collecting their children from the private schools in Headington and traffic edged along bumper to bumper. The closing of the side roads known locally as LTNs, Low Traffic Neighbourhoods, meant there were no longer any short cuts.

'At this rate, it'll be quicker to walk.' They were in an unmarked car but Kate felt she had no alternative but to put on the siren. Even then it wasn't easy without risking an accident but ten minutes later they were parked up and walking into the Maternity Wing.

Reception rang Gynaecology to see if the consultant, Mr Darcy Moss, was in the building.

'He's just finished his outpatients' clinic and can see you now.'

When the consultant greeted her, Kate struggled not to stereotype Mr. Darcy Moss. He was fit and elegantly dressed with a look straight out of a fifties movie. It was not so much his appearance as the clipped tone of voice which made her feel uncomfortable.

'I believe Dr Yasmin Bell worked in your team, Mr Moss.'

'Indeed, she works here but today is not her day in.'

He peered at Kate over his glasses and said

'You will find her at the Nuffield Price Lab on Wednesdays. Reception can direct you.'

He went to open the door to show them out.

'I'm sorry Sir, but you can't have heard the news. Her body was found two nights ago. Her parents have been informed, so it will be reported in the local papers and on Radio Oxford, today.'

Kate looked into the eyes of Mr Darcy Moss. He didn't appear shocked.

'You say her body was found. Was she involved in a traffic accident?'

'No, Sir. She was murdered.'

Veronica Chen was surprised by Kate's abrupt manner. Moss seemed to be affected by the news.

'Who on earth would do ...' and he sat down and didn't finish his sentence.

'That is what we need to find out and we'd appreciate your help.'

'Anything...' this time in a more natural voice.

'Can you tell us exactly what her role was here and whether any patients may have a grudge against her?'

'You are probably aware that Obstetrics and Gynaecology comes with risks of expensive claims if anything goes wrong.'

'But Yasmin hasn't been in any complaints. She occasionally assisted normal deliveries. She was not involved in much surgery on her own. She assisted me in Caesareans and gynaecological operations...' He hesitated.

'But... She carries out abortions on her own. I'm Catholic and withdraw myself from those procedures.'

'I understand there have been some unwanted demonstrations regarding terminations,' said Kate.

'That's correct but I suggest you to talk to her colleague, Dr Jim Azad, on that subject.'

Chen glanced at Kate and repeated the name emphasising the 'Jim'.

'A friend of hers in Thames Reach suggested that she had a relationship with him. Were you aware of it?'

'They were undoubtedly close but I'm not sure that it was a sexual relationship. There didn't appear to be much chemistry between them but you'd better ask him.'

'We understand that Dr Bell's appointment was combined NHS and Oxford University. That she was also involved in research.'

'That's right. We have a well-established project looking into the possibilities of Gene Editing. Again, it's not something I want to be involved in. It's controversial.'

'Why is that?' asked Veronica.

'Even you must have heard of Dolly the Sheep. That was cloning not changing genes. Do you understand the difference?'

Once again a demeaning tone entered his voice. Kate wasn't sure if it was because they were policewomen or just women that they could be talked down to. Chen didn't react apart from taking out her notebook.

'Many of us thought cloning defied church teaching. The first operation to alter a gene in a human took place in 2017. A man in Arizona was given the experimental treatment to try to correct a defect in his DNA that causes Hunter's syndrome. Yasmin was excited because the UK has become the first country in the world to approve gene editing as a potential cure for two inherited blood disorders. Recently a one-year old child received gene editing treatment to help her fight leukaemia. It was successful but some people, myself included, think that genes should be left to the Almighty. But Yasmin was an 'enthusiast.' She could only see the potential for good.'

There was that patronising edge again – the manner in which he said 'enthusiast' with contempt in his voice. It reminded her of the way she had witnessed some female colleagues in the MET being put down for showing any sense of compassion or passion. Moss stood up.

'I'm sorry but I must terminate this interview. I'm a busy man. I'll walk with you to administration and ask them to give you copies of her records. Anything I can do to help find the villain who did this – my door is always open – when not in clinics or the operating theatre.'

'Oh and Dr Azad isn't on the ward today. He is working at the Nuffield Price Lab.'

'Thanks for your help,' said DI Veronica Chen.

Kate gave her email address to the manager so that they could send Yasmin's files digitally.

The Nuffield Price Lab was on the same campus as the hospital. So they walked the two hundred yards to see if they could talk to Dr Azad.

***

Dr Azad was called to reception. He was about 5.8 with jet black hair, a black beard and large dark eyes which resembled Osama Bin Laden's. Kate called herself to order. She was being guilty of stereotyping which she abhorred in others.

Kate asked if there was a room where they could talk in private. Once the door was shut and they were seated, Kate began.

'Dr Azad. I am sorry but we are bearers of sad news. Your colleague Yasmin Bell was found dead on Monday evening.'

Jim Azad looked shaken.

'But how?'

'We are sorry to tell you that it was not of natural causes. She was murdered. We've been told that you and Yasmin were good friends'.

He struggled to say anything. It was as if he was trying to open his mouth and nothing could come out.

'Take your time, Dr Azad. The news will have come as a dreadful shock, but I'm sure you will want to help us find who was responsible.'

He nodded. Kate was trying hard to describe the look on his face. Shock horror 'yes' - but there was something else that she couldn't quite put her finger on.

'You're right we are .. were..' Azad came to halt and put his face in his hands.

Kate looked at Veronica and she nodded.

'Dr Azad, we badly need to talk to you but we can see how upset you are so are happy to come back in the morning. Do you want us to come here or to your home?'

'My home would be better.'

***

Azad lived in a rented flat in a house in Stapleton Road in Headington. In Kate's eyes it didn't look lived in. There were hardly any personal effects and no books which she thought strange. He noticed her looking around.

'I need a place to sleep but most of my waking hours are spent in the lab.'

'Yasmin has a house so I suppose you were able to meet her there?'

'I need to explain that we were not in a relationship.'

'We were told that you met at least twice a week.'

'That's true. We are ... friends but it wasn't a sexual relationship. We usually met over a meal somewhere we could talk in private.'

Kate sensed a nervousness or was it *fear* that she'd read in his expression yesterday?

'We both work on the same research project and it helped to discuss it in private.'

Kate looked sympathetic.

'I know that feeling all too well and sympathise. You can imagine that Veronica –DI Chen and I need to let off steam occasionally.'

'Then you understand the relationship between Yasmin and me.'

'When did you meet?' asked DI Chen.

'We met here in Oxford working on the same wards. Now I work full time on research. Last summer we attended a conference in the USA together and yes, we liked each other and found we had a great deal in common.'

'Can you tell us more?'

'We have our work and research interests in common and we

are both culturally Muslim. My father is an Iranian born Shiite but my mother was born here and her background is Sunni. That's unusual. Yasmin's mother is Iranian but her father is British and culturally Christian. Our parents are not religious but they value their heritage. There are issues we both encountered growing up in this country with our background - assumptions made about us ...'

Kate felt an inner blush. Even she had been momentarily guilty of that when she first saw Jim Azad.

'It's good that you had each other to talk to,' said Kate.

'Yes. We were able to talk on private matters and things that concerned us.'

'Which were?' prodded Kate.

It looked as if he was going to continue in an open way but Kate noticed a wary look cross his face. He paused before answering.

'Work issues mostly.'

'Which work issues?'

Once again he paused before replying.

'To do with time pressures, research that sort of thing.'

Kate sensed there was something he wasn't telling them but they weren't going to get much more out of him, today. They would have to do some digging. Maybe Steve Darwin could help with that.

Chapter 7

Some of Alex's friends thought her strangely old fashioned because she had printed newspapers delivered and loved libraries. Being self-employed and an author, she liked to indulge herself first thing in the morning. A slow breakfast reading a real paper and doing the Guardian crossword was a daily pleasure. It was fellow crime writer, Colin Dexter, who introduced her to that and more.

When Alex moved from London knowing few people in Oxford, work as a freelance writer for *The Oxford Times* introduced her to the rich cultural life of her new home. When she interviewed Colin, she was astonished to discover that he'd written most of the Inspector Morse books while working full time at the Oxford Delegacy. She'd asked him,

'But how? How did you it?'

'It was like this. I came home for supper, listened to the Archers and went to the pub for a pint or two but I'd worked out that there are 365 days in a year and if I wrote a page a day, I'd have written a book.'

Alex had begun by emulating his daily discipline to write her first Whodunit *Bad Blood in Summertown.* The success of that led her to try crosswords too. She hoped that planting hidden clues would enhance her writing. It was no surprise that Dexter named his detective after a fellow Oxford crossword compiler, Jonathan Morse. It wasn't the crossword puzzle in *The Oxford Times* that gained her attention but the front page. She was looking at a picture of Yasmin Bell in front of a white board giving a lecture.

Hospital doctor found murdered on Boars Hill

The police were called to Chandlings Manor School shortly after 21:30 GMT on Monday evening. Local residents taking part in the amphibian rescue service known as Toad Patrol found the body of Dr Yasmin Bell near the school's lake. The police are treating it as murder. Chief Inspector Ranjit Singh says,

'Incidents such as this are tragic and disturbing and will cause distress in the community. Yasmin was much loved. We are confident that the community will want to help us find who did this. If you have any information, however small, even if you think it isn't relevant, please ring the number below or message us. (It appeared on the screen in the TV news)

'Yasmin's father is the historian and former diplomat Professor Jonathan Bell. Professor Bell is well known for fronting historical documentary series for Channel 4. His wife Nasreen is Iranian and was forced into exile for campaigning for women's rights.

'Yasmin was a popular member of staff at the John Radcliffe Hospital. She was also involved in the gene editing research project at the Nuffield Price Laboratory. She lived in Thames Reach since November 2023.'

Alex didn't regard herself as devious but she had woken up figuring out ways to meet Steve Darwin. She could call on Sam anytime and hope to cross his path but the house and the gym and annex were now separate. It was only if he wanted a swim that she was likely to meet him. From his photo, Steve looked like he preferred food to physical exercise. That gave her an idea. Alex telephoned Sam. When she ended the call, there was a smile on her face for the first time since that fateful evening. She went to her bookcases and removed a volume titled *The Wonder of Life*, put it in her bag and headed out of the house in the direction of Abingdon Way.

Chapter 8

While Kate was interviewing Jim Azad in his sparsely furnished rented flat, Ranjit headed for Woodland Road. He had the Bell's permission to search Yasmin's house. As he was looking for number 129, he saw in his rear view mirror Alex Hornby walking briskly in the same direction.

He parked up and waited to speak to her.

'DI Jordan and I are going to take a look at Yasmin's house. Does the crime writer have any clues?' he asked with a grin.

Alex's good mood disintegrated.

'That comment isn't in good taste given that I found poor Yasmin's body. I can't forget what I've seen.'

'I have to find some humour or I couldn't do this job. In my career, I've seen horrific sights at the scene of car accidents and gas explosions but this horror was deliberate. You've been diligent in not describing it to anyone so I'd like to give you some information that may help a bit. The Forensic Pathologist's report came in this morning. The good news, if you can describe it that way, is that she was dead before the surgery. She was drugged. The pathologist can't be certain that she wasn't conscious but, if she wasn't already dead, what happened to her would have been through a haze and without pain. The umbilical cord was not the cause of death, more for decoration.'

'I really appreciate you telling me that. Thank you. Thank you very much. I've usually been a good sleeper but I've had to take sleeping pills this week. As soon as I put my head on the pillow, I see her.'

'You and me both. We must get on with the job of finding out who did this.'

Ranjit opened the gate of 129 but then turned,

'If you get any ideas about who hated her that much, get in touch. I think you have my number but here's my card anyway.'

Alex nodded and waved goodbye. She knew, from Kate, that he'd joked about her in the Price case and felt a bit threatened by her. That conversation had taken some doing on his part.

***

It was March 2 and still pretty chilly.

'The central heating must be on a timer because the house is warm,' Ranjit said to Peter. The kitchen was clean and tidy. A half-filled cafetiere was on the work top and a half-drunk mug of coffee next to it. They bagged the mug just in case. Peter opened the dishwasher. It was loaded but it was hard to know whether the dishes had been accumulated over a couple of days or she'd shared her final lunch.'

Jim Azad had received a call from her at 10 am on her last day, saying she was going to work from home and then go for a run before lunch but would be in the lab after 4pm. The hunt for her phone and laptop was on. The house had not been trashed and there was no evidence of a break-in, but after an hour of looking they gave up the search for the devices. Given the lack of disturbance, had Yasmin let her killer in? No keys had been found. Had the murderer taken them? Ranjit had used her parents set. But he was struggling to find evidence that the murderer had killed her in the house and then moved the body.

Once they were in the car, Ranjit turned to Peter and said,

'The Greeks w0uld say that the gods are not favouring us. We can send in a team to look for finger prints, but the odds of finding any of interest are low.'

Chapter 9

Number 1 Abingdon Way was no longer a fortress. The gates were wide open; the barbed wire and security cameras had gone. A pair of olive trees in large terracotta pots stood either side of the front door. Alex rang the bell. Professor Steve Darwin opened it. He looked surprised but not annoyed. Alex held out her hand

'Professor Darwin, I'm Alex Hornby, a friend of Sam. Can I come in, please?'

He ushered her into the open plan lounge, diner and kitchen area.

'What can I do for you?'

'I hope there is something I can do for you but yes, I do have a request.'

'Thames Reach is a friendly village once you make an effort but, as you are only here for six months, some of us would like to show you around, if that interests you?'

Alex opened her bag and took out her copy of *The Wonder of Life* by Steve Darwin.

'I'd love you to sign this.'

'Delighted. You'd better come in. I'll make us some coffee,' said a smiling Steve Darwin.

Over coffee she said,

'Would the Friends of Radley Large Wood interest you? Given your fame, your support could help us a lot...' and their eyes connected.

Again that charming smile: it made him look youthful. Kate tried to remember how old he was. She had an idea it was around sixty-six.

'So tell me about it?' said Steve.

'The recommended management of ancient woodland is that

only ten per cent should be felled in five years. The new owners have felled that much in three months. We are desperate to maintain the biodiversity of the woods, the carpets of wild flowers, the network of fungi, the birds, bats, and badgers. The new owners are St. Hilda's college. We don't think they are listening to us: it looks like they prefer the message of the industrial foresters they have appointed which focuses on felling and replanting. But they may listen to you?'

Steve was not unused to protest during his sixty-seven years on this earth.

***

Once back home, Alex posted the good news on the Friends of Radley Large Wood WhatsApp Group. 'Steve Darwin said 'Yes'. Meet this Sunday morning at 11am at the Pavilion ready to walk across the Memorial Field to show him the woods.

What she didn't say was that she had arranged for Steve and herself to have lunch at the Kings Arms next to the Thames afterwards.

***

Later that afternoon, DS Farr and DI Chen also knocked on the door of 1 Abingdon Way. They'd arranged to talk to Professor Darwin. But before they left the station they did a quick check that he was as he'd said on a plane from Boston USA when Yasmin was murdered. His alibi checked out.

'I'm sorry this wasn't the welcome you expected, Professor Darwin, but I hope you understand why we need to talk to you?' said DS Kate Farr.

He nodded and replied,

'I met Yasmin Bell in person at a conference at Harvard in

June last year. My expertise is in evolution and the brain. Yasmin and her colleague, Jim Azad, came to talk about the project they were working on about gene editing. You may wonder why that interests me? *Whether this new environment is going to lead to evolutionary changes* is up for question.'

'Why was it you kept in touch?'

'It was Yasmin who emailed me for advice. Since then we had a couple of brief WhatsApp chats but mostly communicated by email. You're right of course; I couldn't imagine this would happen to her.'

'But you said she was disturbed about something?'

'There were a few things. As I didn't know Yasmin well, it's hard to know which worried her the most. It's a brief acquaintance but I have kept the emails – about six, I think.'

Steve opened his laptop and searched 'Yasmin Bell' and a chain of emails emerged. Here's the first which is not about her research - it's about Serena Shriver.

Dear Steve,

There is a woman called Serena Shriver in Oxford. She's anti-abortion. I understand people who are anti-abortion. My boss Darcy Moss is, but we agree to disagree. Serena thinks differently and led a US vigil near our abortion clinic. It upset our patients who were jostled on their way in and placards waved in their faces – you know the kind of placards. The reason I'm emailing you is for your advice and opinion. Her son Gideon was quite threatening. Should I take it seriously?

I hope you make it to Oxford. If you want accommodation, there's a lovely AirB&B available near where I live.'

'In my career, I've been involved in many campaigns and demonstrations even right here in Oxford. I was here, decades ago, as an undergraduate, when there were demonstrations outside a barber's shop in the Cowley Road. You had to be white for him to cut your hair... a bit of Apartheid in Oxford. But we didn't want barbers dead. They have the right to demonstrate but threatening doctors is another level.'

Steve continued.

'Times have changed – oh to be young again. I rented a house in this village when I was doing my DPhil. At that time, there was just one resident who wasn't white, an academic at Oxford Polytechnic. He shared my interests. I've noticed a difference. Thames Reach is bigger and no longer quite so white, evidenced by an attractive black woman who called on me this morning.'

'Was that my friend Alex Hornby?' asked Kate.

'Why yes. Does everyone know everyone else in Thames Reach?'

'Do you mind if we get back to your correspondence with Yasmin. You said she was interested in Serena Shriver of the Republican National Coalition for Life.'

'That's right. Her son Gideon is studying theology at Oxford. He accosted Yasmin when she was leaving the hospital and threatened her. He and his mother organised a US style demonstration against abortion. She wanted to know whether she should take it seriously because he appeared to be serious.'

'What did you advise?'

'I couldn't tell her not to be concerned but this is England and, unlike in the USA, the fundamentalists don't have much support here. In the States, the lives of many doctors who perform abortions are difficult. Right wing Republicans have made it into a political crusading issue. They're making gains. Rowe v Wade that gave all women the right to a termination was overturned. Now it's down to the individual states and many have banned abortions.

To think this happened under a President with a reputation for being a sex pest!

'You'll see in the email chain that I advised her not to respond in a political manner. Keep the tone measured and medical. Don't respond angrily as that will encourage them.'

'You said there was more than one issue.'

'A month ago she got in touch. She thought she was being followed and wondered if it could be related to her research because her computer had been hacked and some data had gone missing.'

'That seemed worrying so I suggested she report it to you: the police. Did she?'

'Maybe she would be alive today, if she had reported it; although the force doesn't always respond quickly in cases of stalking.'

'Yasmin seemed more cheerful when I told her that I was coming to Oxford for six months to work with Gavin McGeorge. She recommended this house. It's a bit large for me on my own but my son and his family are coming for a holiday after schools break up. This place can house them.'

'What do you think of Jim Azad?'

'I can't say that I know him – I've met him, but that's not *knowing* someone. I only met Yasmin face to face at the conference last June but I have a strong sense of her as a person.'

'Can you describe her to me?'

'Passionate, energetic, hard-working and committed to women's rights. Some of that must come from her mother. You know about her?'

'Nasreen came with her husband to identify the body. We questioned them for fifteen minutes afterwards. More than that felt inappropriate at that moment in time. It's hard to imagine how it must feel to have to see the dead body of your only child. I asked if Yasmin had talked to them about being stalked. The answer was 'No' and that deeply upset them. From body language, I felt that it was completely news to the father but maybe not as much of a surprise to Nasreen. I've asked to interview her again.'

'Look at this email, said Steve.

'My mother's regarded as a threat by the Revolutionary Guard. When she speaks at public meetings, she has a shrewd idea of who they've planted to record her. After one meeting, two men deliberately bumped in to us when we were walking to a restaurant. They said 'sorry' but didn't move out of the way in a hurry. One of them reached inside his jacket to reveal a bulge which my mother believed was a gun. Last year, I helped some feminist scientists escape from Iran. I got accreditation for them at a medical conference in Cairo. They were allowed to attend but had 'chaperones'. We managed to get them out of the ladies loo through a window and to the US embassy where they applied for asylum. Despite that, I don't think it's them following me.'

'Yasmin asked the embassy to contact me and they did. But they didn't need much persuading that they were genuine asylum seekers.'

Chapter 10

For the end of day briefing, Ranjit described his visit to the victim's house and his suspicion of a targeted burglary – computers and mobile devices.

'The forensics team are going over the place as we speak. As her laptop has been taken, we need to have access to her computer at the Nuffield Price Lab and whatever you can get from the server, Richard. In the meantime we have some of her emails and in particular her correspondence with Professor Darwin.'

When DS Farr sat down after reporting on her interview with Steve Darwin, the meeting looked as if they were overwhelmed and that this case was developing into political territory beyond their experience. Peter Jordan asked,

'Should we be reporting this to MI6?'

'Fair question, but I want to delay that until we get a better sense of the whole story. Once we involve them, they will take over and the 'local' will be relegated. Would the Iranians really mutilate her body like that? I doubt it. They would be more likely to employ a hit man. Their Russian allies would poison her but the actual method of execution seems personal, don't you think? 'replied Ranjit.

Kate was not convinced. She was turning over ideas in her head like 'If someone wanted to divert attention from the real culprits they'd succeeded – and then there was Jim Azad? Yasmin regarded him as a close friend but something Steve Darwin said rang alarm bells. *I met him but that doesn't mean that I know him.*

Ranjit had directed his question at Kate and Veronica.

'Sorry Sir, can you repeat that?' asked Ranjit.

'Since DI Chen heard my question, she can answer it.'

'I followed up with Dr Azad early this morning and have some interesting things to report. The atmosphere near the hospital and the labs has been disturbed by recent demonstrations against abortion led by Serena Shriver. He said some of the poison from the States was spreading over here. Yasmin and one of her colleagues had received some hate mail. Oddly none was sent to male members of staff only to his female colleagues. He also said that, a few months ago, she asked to be moved to a different consultant.

'Dr Azad said "I'm not sure that it was so much about him as a nurse in the team that concerned her. Barbara Covet. Yasmin was present at a delivery and said that instead of disposing of the umbilical cord the usual way, Yasmin believed she'd put it in a bag and removed it from the operating theatre."'

'Well, that needs following up. Well done Chen. See what Nurse Covet has to say for herself.'

Chapter 11

While Chen and a constable headed for the JR to find out what they could about Nurse Covet, Ranjit decided to accompany Kate to the interview with Nasreen. Jonathan Bell answered the door and behind him, coming down the stairs, was his wife dressed from head to toe in black with thick black circles beneath her eyes where she had been crying. Kate thought how different she looked from the Google images she had scrolled through where Nasreen wore bright colours and usually had her hair loose. It was as if she had become a conservative Muslim.

No sooner had they sat down than Nasreen asked,

'When will Yasmin's body be released for burial? I may not be a regular worshipper but I am culturally Muslim and am used to having funerals immediately.'

'I'm so sorry. I'll try and make sure that can happen soon. We would like to attend the funeral.'

'We want the burial to be just be for immediate family but we shall organise a memorial to Yasmin for her colleagues and friends and our friends. Jonathan wants it to be in Worcester College Chapel. Do you know it?'

'Not well but my near neighbour, the author Alex Hornby effused about it after she worked for a day as an extra on the film '& Sons...' Kate stopped abruptly. She was aware that the scene with Bill Nighy was a funeral in the chapel. That scene focused on an old man nearing the end of his life but the Bell memorial occasion would be for a bright and beautiful young woman whose real potential would never be achieved. Kate changed the subject.

'When we asked you if Yasmin had talked about being followed, you both replied 'No' but, it looked as if it didn't come as a complete surprise to you, Mrs Bell.'

'You're right. I have experience of being followed. What do you know about Iran, detectives?'

Kate looked at Ranjit.

'It's predominately Shia Muslim.'

Nasreen looked disappointed. Then Kate followed up on the question.

'As a woman I've followed the protests against the dress codes and have learned a lot from your speeches.'

Her emphasis was on *'your'*.

'For instance, I didn't know that under the Iranian penal code, the age of criminal responsibility for women is just nine years, compared with fifteen years for men.'

'That's right, and the discrimination is throughout the legal system. Women receive harsher punishments than men for several crimes, including adultery. Most sentences of death by stoning for adultery are levelled against women. The penalties for minor infringement of the dress code can be incarceration in prisons where torture is the norm,' said Nasreen Bell.

'Yasmin was excited by the Women Life Freedom uprising. She was optimistic that things were going to change. The young generation in Iran are at one, united in their desire for a freer life. So when the demonstrations were met not with reform but a brutal crackdown, she was heartbroken. Yasmin can speak Farsi....'

Nasreen choked as she realised she had used the present tense.

'She had been corresponding with some young Iranian scientists. I think you know that she helped one of them get asylum in the USA.'

Ranjit nodded.

'She was a courageous young woman. I understand why you are so proud of her.'

'But when things like that happen the regime intimidates friends and family into silence. Even in this country the Revolutionary

Guard has its tentacles. I've been trying to uncover the identity of one of their agents based here in Oxford. Not that our government is doing much more than utter words of concern. I wouldn't put it past them to have had a hand in Yasmin's death for what she did and as revenge against me.'

Kate's saw the loss of hope in Nasreen Bell's eyes. She wanted to reassure her that they would at least find the killer and bring him to justice. She was convinced it was a man but now she wasn't so sure that they would find him. If he was an agent of the Iranian state, he was as likely to escape justice as the Salisbury poisoners. They were living it up as heroes in Moscow. She was experiencing one of her sceptical episodes, but she'd never share her doubts with her colleagues.

***

Back at the station, Ranjit was considering whether he should contact the Secret Services when there was knock on his door. The forensic team had brought a report which made him decide to delay that phone call. A recent blood splatter in the bath room at Yasmin's house made it likely that it was the scene of the murder. The bathroom had been thoroughly cleaned but the splatter was on the underside of a pipe leading to a bidet. The report made clear that it was Yasmin's blood and not menstrual blood. To get where it was found meant it was unlikely to be caused by an accidental graze. Yasmin must have let the murderer in. Could any neighbours have seen any comings and goings? He'd ask Peter to organise a house to house in the vicinity.

DI Chen was knocking on the door.

'Come in.'

'I'm sorry, Sir, but Nurse Covet had a week's leave. Her colleagues say she is visiting family in Wales but is due back at work on Monday.'

'Do we go to Cardiff or wait till then?' mused Ranjit.

'The bureaucracy will be tedious on South Wales' patch and we may get more out of her if she doesn't suspect that we suspect her. Have a good weekend.'

Chapter 12

This was becoming such a complicated case. The Chief Inspector wanted Kate to look into the Serena and her son, Gideon Shriver.

'She saw on the Richmond College website that Serena was booked to preach there on Sunday. Going incognito to the service could be useful before interviewing them?' mused Kate. But she was determined to have some free time at the weekend. So, on Friday night, when Alex rang to suggest a walk in the morning she was keen.

'Meet at Sam's at 11.'

***

Sam's son, Little Goldie, was excited as they crossed the railway bridge.

'Two year olds love trains' thought Alex. Steve did the honours and lifted him out of his stroller to see the green light and watch the London train approaching.

'The year I spent in Oxford while writing my PhD thesis, Jack was the same age as Goldie. This walk brings back good memories. I'm a grandfather now. Jack and his partner Elysia and my nine year old grandson Stu are coming at Easter,' said Steve.

'You'll find that some things have changed for good and others not so good.'

As they walked down the metal steps, Alex pointed ahead of them in the direction of the hard path below.

'That's Sustrans, the National Cycle Trail – an asset. But the lovely old white painted Edwardian college boat on this stretch of the Thames, where families could watch their children rowing in Eights Week, has been broken up. I miss surprising encounters with history, but let's take you to Sandford Lasher.'

They turned left off of Sustrans and crossed two fields avoiding some muddy patches. Once at their destination Alex couldn't help herself: she embarked on a mini history lesson of how Thames Reach was a favourite place, on hot sunny days, for Victorian students to ride or walk to, drink at the pub, picnic and swim.

'And this is where 'Peter Pan' drowned.'

'Did Captain Hook make him walk the plank?' grinned Steve.

Alex looked a little embarrassed but laughed.

'Your compatriot, Jerome K Jerome, said that it was "the perfect place to drown yourself in", but Michael's adopted father, JM Barrie, was heartbroken. He wasn't alone among Christ Church students to die here.'

Alex pointed to the obelisk the college had built in their memory.

'But look that's a new and positive sight. That wasn't here when you stayed that time.' Alex pointed out that the local hydro-electric scheme made use of the powerful current using slowly turning Archimedes screws. Darwin said,

'That's what I like about Oxford: history, literature, science all converge here.'

They headed for lunch at the Kings Arms, but Sam excused herself.

'I like Goldie to keep to a bit of routine. It makes my life a lot easier, so I'll say goodbye and take him home for an afternoon nap. Enjoy your lunch.'

***

Twenty minutes later, Steve, Alex and Kate were sitting by a window in the Kings Arms looking through delicate branches of weeping willow towards Sandford Lock.

'This is such a beautiful place but I can't help but associate it with the death of Sam's husband. At least he had experienced a long life, had children and grandchildren but Yasmin is different: such a tragic loss,' said Kate.

As she was talking, a man at the bar turned his head. It was her colleague, Peter Jordan. Kate looked despairingly at Alex,

'I bet Peter will tell my boss that I'm having a friendly lunch with you and talking about the case.'

Kate was feeling uneasy about her work colleagues. Ranjit had improved in the way he talked about her in front of her colleagues but, between them, the undermining remarks had not been eliminated altogether. She sometimes wondered if he felt threatened by her. She hadn't known that Chen had returned to Azad before she reported back to the team meeting. Kate wondered if she was being shut out.

It was Steve who noticed that she was genuinely worried.

'Tell them you are conferring with the best brains, not meaning me, but Alex here. Who better to solve this case than a crime writer?' said Steve.

'That's the problem. Not over the moon about it.'

Alex described her encounter with Ranjit outside Yasmin's house.

'Maybe he's rethinking a bit, Kate?'

Their meal arrived. Although they all enjoyed it and the company, Alex couldn't help thinking that she preferred the cuisine of her parents' birthplace, the West Indies. Life felt more exciting with a touch of spice. She found herself suggesting that they come to her next weekend and she'd cook her version of Jamaican Jerk chicken and Indian Aloo Tikka chaat. It was agreed. Kate looked forward to Alex's lovingly prepared food. Once home from a long shift, she rarely cooked and she was in no doubt that the micro-waved meals she relied on were not good for her.

'I've promised to walk with the Radley Great Wood campaigners next Sunday, but I can make it by one o'clock' said Steve. 'I believe you two and Yasmin also supported the campaign.'

Kate's abundant red curly hair fell across her face. She swept it behind her ears. Steve looked admiringly at it.

'Your hair suits you loose like that,' he said.

'In my work, its best if it looks severe and untouchable! That's why I tie it so tightly back.'

Alex looked sympathetic.

'An advantage with braids is that they stay put!'

'All this talk of hair! I wish I had some to boast of,' laughed Steve.

Alex leant forward and touched a Tin Tin like tuft.

'Ooh' thought Kate, 'that was intimate.'

She felt a twinge of envy. Since her divorce, she had tried a dating app but soon realised that it wasn't for her. She needed a connection in life as she lived it. That meant there was a void which she filled with work.

They walked back to Thames Reach via the Thames Path and talked more openly about the murder out of earshot of Peter Jordan.

Kate said, 'Gideon Shriver is studying at Richmond College. It's a Baptist foundation.'

Alex added her bit of history and didn't apologise either.

'For hundreds of years, you had to be an Anglican to study in Oxford. It wasn't opened to Catholics or non-conformists. Only in 1871 were religious tests completely abolished. Richmond was founded in the nineteen thirties, so a young college by Oxford standards.'

'Gideon's mother is going to preach there tomorrow. I thought I might go. I'm down to interview them on Monday. I'll introduce

myself after the service and be polite and book a convenient time,'
said Kate.

'Would you like me to come with you?' suggested Alex.

'Would you? I'd love that. Any advice for me, Steve?'

'Think a modern day version of Phyllis Schafly.'

Steve realised that Kate had no idea who that was.

'Watch 'Mrs America' if it's still streaming. Remember I'm a palaeontologist and Phyllis sure was a dinosaur. You could describe her opinions as *paleoconservative*.'

Alex took out her notebook and wrote the word down.

'I can use that to describe a character in my latest novel.'

'Phyllis was opposed to feminism, gay rights, and abortion, and campaigned against the Equal Rights Amendment to the U.S. Constitution. Serena is her 2025 equivalent. She wants women back in the kitchen. Think Nazi Germany's attitude of 'kinder küche kirche'! The way Serena puts it is "women at the heart of the home." I'd take bets that her sermon will be about family values.'

Chapter 13

Alex's mother had been a committed Christian and Pentecostal church attendance had been a regular feature of her childhood. After arriving from Jamaica, her mother Grace and father Bernard had set off for their local Anglican church.

Chatting to Kate on the way into Oxford, Alex said,

'They were welcomed with an icy cold bath of hostility. The vicar was upset and asked some of his congregation why they hadn't spoken to Grace and Bernard. The answer was 'Black people moving into the district will devalue our property.'

Kate wasn't surprised.

'But you said you were taken to church every Sunday?'

'Not only my parents, but most Christian black Britons experienced a similar cold shoulder so they came together to form their own churches. My parents weren't happy-clappy and would've preferred the Anglican way to Pentecostal rapture but they enjoyed the support and the friendship.'

***

The atmosphere in the chapel was warm and welcoming. Alex looked comfortable. The college chaplain conducted most of the service and introduced Serena to give the address. She looked elegant as she walked gracefully to the pulpit.

'Thank you for inviting me to speak today. I feel honoured that my son Gideon has been welcomed into this esteemed college. We have much to share and together we are stronger.

'The devil can be charming and all of us can be tempted. We should not be ashamed of that. Our Lord Jesus himself was tempted...'

This wasn't going the way Kate thought it would. She was

beginning to think that coming was a waste of time, when she noticed a few rows ahead, on the other side of the aisle, was non other that the JR consultant, Mr Darcy Moss! Her mind started to wander until the name of the new Vice President of the USA, JD Vance was mentioned. Alex whispered in her ear,

'Cat ladies!'

Serena's voice had become more determined but somehow maintained a soft, feminine tone.

'Life is sacred, even life within the womb so I welcome his willingness to fight the good fight and stand up for the liberties of religious Britons. You will need courage and even a thick skin because the opposition will be aggressive, but gird your loins and know that God is with you. And may the Lord bless you and may his light shine upon you and give you strength. Amen'

After the final hymn and grace, the chaplain invited the congregation for tea and coffee and to meet Serena. Kate noticed that Moss and Shriver were side by side as they walked to the hall where refreshments were to be served. Kate quickly took some photos on her phone.

They helped themselves to coffee and moved to the side. Kate went up to them.

'What a pleasure to see you here, Mr Moss.'

'It's Detective Sergeant Farr, if I remember correctly?'

'Good memory, Mr Moss. It's convenient for me that you are here together,' said Kate.

Looking Serena in the eye,

'Two birds with one stone – sorry for the cliché. But I needed to contact you tomorrow to set up formal interviews regarding the murder of Dr Yasmin Bell.'

If they were not pleased, they didn't show it but exuded charm and appointments were made for Tuesday 11 March.

'Serena is staying with me, so you're welcome to interview

us at my house on Boars Hill: Berkley Mansion near the Peking University campus. I'll be home early on Tuesday so 5pm will suit us.' There was an edge to 'Peking'.

When they left, Alex and Kate headed for Dishoom's for a spicy lunch. While tucking into the spinach chaat, Alex said,

'Darcy doesn't hide his disapproval of the sale of the Open University site to the Chinese.'

'I heard that too,' said Kate.

Darcy wasn't alone. The Chinese bent over backwards to be friendly. Nowadays, I often walk around the lake there but when it was owned by the Open University, it was closed to the public. The Peking University campus wanted to provide a free mini-bus and open their cafeteria to walkers and residents but, like my parents, they received an icy cold reception.'

***

Kate and Alex had agreed to join the Radley Large Wood campaigners for an inspection walk there in the afternoon. After their colourful lunch, they headed straight to the Playing Fields to meet George Gamble and some other members of the Friends of Radley Large Wood. They had walking books, hats and scarves ready in Alex's car.

Alex introduced Kate to the others. The eight of them included experts on badgers, bats, reptiles, trees, and flora. As they walked Alex explained to Kate.

'What's special about these woods is the abundance of wild flowers. When I first walked here in spring it felt like the birth of paradise. You'll see the celandines and wood anemones will be coming into bloom. You need arboreal cover for decades for them to carpet the ground. This woodland is ancient and was once owned by the Abbot of...'Alex paused.

'Here I go again. I can't stop rabbiting on about history.'

'That's what surprises me. You write crime fiction but I'd have thought historical fiction would be your niche,' said Kate.

That conversation came to an end when they reached the gate to the woods. They walked first in the untouched areas, took photos and then headed along the path parallel to the Memorial Field. After eight minutes the vista changed. No trees - just a sea of mud.

'I see why you're upset, George,' said Kate, who was seeing the damage for the first time. Merryn, the badger expert, took them as near as they could to the sett but the deep ruts filled with water made it hard to reach.

'It's going to take some time cleaning our boots,' said Kate. 'Lucky we have clean shoes in the car.'

Once pictures were taken they headed back to the car park.

'Would you like a lift, George? In fact why not come and have tea with us?' suggested Alex.

They left their muddy boots in her porch and headed for the kitchen.

'Why don't you two make yourselves comfortable? I've baked scones for a cream tea.'

'I'm sure I've put on weight since I met you, Alex. Serena Shriver would say you are a tempter,' said Kate.

George reacted to the name 'Serena'. Kate had trained herself to notice body language so asked him,

'Have you met her?

'Yes, and not in nice circumstances. Yasmin Bell lived opposite me and we often met when she went for a run and I was bird watching. A month or so ago, she looked distressed and I asked her what was wrong. You know she worked at the JR.' They nodded.

'She'd been getting nasty emails and ignored them but there was a week when she had to make her way through a barrage of protesters carrying huge placards with graphic images of foetuses. One woman jumped out and threw baby clothes covered in blood at her. Leading the protest was Serena Shriver and her son: they seemed to have inside knowledge when the abortion clinics take place.

'I promised that I'd get some friends to form a barrier at the abortion clinic the following week. We stood in between Serena's baying crowd and the nurses, doctors and patients entering the hospital. Serena shouted at the young women arriving that having an abortion was like putting their baby in a meat grinder.

'Thanks to Yasmin things improved. She led a delegation of medics, nurses and pro-choice activists to the hospital management and told them that what was happening was illegal. She explained that

"This isn't the USA and, in Britain, there has to be a buffer zone." It cost the hospital money they could ill afford to employ security guards to enforce it.'

Kate thanked him. It looked like this was their most promising line of enquiry. They needed to focus on the John Radcliffe and forget Iran.

Chapter 14

Kate and Ranjit had arranged to see the Head of Nursing before meeting Nurse Barbara Covet, now returned from her holiday break. On the drive to the JR, Alex reported the conversation with George and said,

'On Sunday morning, I did something beyond the call of duty and went to hear Serena preach at Richmond College and guess who was there?'

'Sergeant Farr, this isn't Quiz Night on the TV...'

'None other than his smugness Darcy Moss. And guess what?'

'I'm not in the mood to guess, just tell me,' said Ranjit.

'She's only staying with him and I arranged to interview both of them at his house in Boars Hill tomorrow.'

'Boars Hill. Now that is interesting. I'll come with you,' smiled Ranjit.

Ranjit's mood improved as they were shown into Mrs Bellamy, Head of Nursing's office.

'Thank you for agreeing to see us.'

'The whole hospital is shaken by the death of Dr Bell. She was a valued member of staff. Anything we can do to help?'

They started by checking out George's account of the protests and his version checked out.

'We had to act. Patients are distressed before they get here but that reception meant that women were crying in the waiting room and that affected the staff.'

'How did Dr Bell get on with the nursing staff?'

'She was popular.'

'We understand that there was one nurse she had problems with, Barbara Covet?'

When Mrs Bellamy hesitated. Ranjit, knew that his question had landed.

'That is true, but I'm sure it was nothing significant.'

'Let me be the judge of that, please. Did Yasmin make an official complaint against her?'

'She came to see me three weeks ago asking to make an official complaint but I managed to persuade her to wait. I asked her to let me investigate before doing that.'

'What was Dr Bell's complaint?'

'Barbara Covet is a midwife and she felt her bedside manner with patients had something to be desired - a little cold maybe? Dr Bell called it "judgemental". But Barbara is a hardworking and reliable midwife and we have a shortage of midwives.'

Ranjit knew there something she wasn't telling them.

'Was that all? That doesn't seem grounds for of an official complaint. Mrs Bellamy, this is a murder inquiry. Any detail however insignificant you think it is, could be a useful lead.'

'You understand that I have no proof, only Dr Bell's word...'

'And that was?'

'Dr Bell believed she didn't always dispose of the placenta and umbilical cords from patients in the orthodox manner. She believes she may even have taken them out of the hospital.'

'Thank you Mrs Bellamy, you have been helpful. Could you send for Nurse Covet please?'

***

Barbara Covet was wearing a standard pale blue scrub top and trousers. The top was pristine and immaculately ironed. Her pale blond hair was drawn tightly back in a bun and she wore a tiny silver crucifix. There was something about her gait that looked familiar to Kate. She felt sure she had seen Barbara Covet somewhere.

'Thank you for coming. I'm sure you aren't surprised by our visit. We need to talk to everyone with whom Dr Bell had been in touch before her murder.'

Barbara said nothing.

'Please sit down.'

'You understand that there is a question we have to ask every-one involved in Yasmin Bell's life:

'Where were you on 28 Feb?'

'I was due a holiday because I had worked over Christmas and the New Year. I was on my way to Wales.'

'Where were you going?'

'To Cardiff, to see my parents.'

'How did you travel?'

'By car.'

'Write down the registration of the car you were driving and give it to DS Farr, please.'

Kate was surprised when Ranjit brought the interview to a swift end without mentioning the accusation against her.

***

Walking back to the car, he said,

'It should be easy to check her story. There's plenty of CCTV on the M4. Get Richard to check out her alibi.'

Kate took out her phone and was about to ring Richard but Ranjit continued,

'I could see you were surprised when I terminated the interview. I don't want it known that we are interested in the umbilical cord. There could be others who knew she had it. I'd rather she didn't think that we suspect her – not until we have more on her.'

'Yes Sir. I feel sure that I've met her before.'

Kate looked at her and scrolled down some pics she had taken on Sunday of Darcy and Serena together and of the congregation. That crucifix ... there it was.

'Sir, look at this. That's her. With her hair half over one side of her face and that bright red coat and dangly earrings, she looked so different from in her uniform but that's her. And she knows Serena and Moss.'

'Well done Sergeant. There are so many strands to this investigation that it felt like a confusing mess but we seem to be getting somewhere. Let's see what Serena Shriver and Darcy Moss have to say for themselves.'

Chapter 15

Ranjit and Kate drove past the Bells' house on Foxcombe Road and turned right towards the Peking University Campus and Yarn Mound. It reminded Kate and Ranjit of visiting an estate agent there while investigating the murder of Godfrey Price. The Moss Mansion was diagonally opposite behind tall metal gates. Kate got out and pressed the intercom. A woman answered, a woman with a local Oxfordshire timbre, nothing like Darcy's plummy voice. She opened the gates.

The housekeeper ushered them in saying,

'Would you like to wait in the lounge and I'll fetch Mrs Shriver.'

'Thank you, Mrs?'

'Mrs Cobb. I'm Mr Moss's housekeeper.'

'Do you live in?'

'No my dear, I live in Thames Reach.'

'Are you here every day?'

'Oh no. The hours suit me well. I work here four days a week from 11-7. I cook and clean and generally manage the house. I leave meals for Mr Moss on the days when I'm here. The other days he eats out. He likes to dine in his old college at least once a week. '

'How long have you worked for him?'

'Nearly four years.'

'Have you always worked as a housekeeper? How does he compare to some of your previous employers? ' asked Kate.

'Oh no. This is my first housekeeping job. I was made redundant when Debenhams closed. I'd worked there since my children became old enough to be left on their own. At 58, there were not many opportunities. This suits me just fine. I feel like I'm my own boss. I don't see much of Mr Moss and he doesn't interfere. He's at the JR and the Abbey four days a week and on Tuesdays when he works from home, he rarely comes out of his study.'

'Thank you Mrs Cobb. You know that we want to interview your boss after we've finished with Mrs Shriver. By the way, when did she arrive here?' said Kate.

'She came at the middle of January, at the start of term and then left for a week. I think she stayed in London. She's been here from the end of January.' She paused and added, 'apart from only a few days at a conference in Cardiff.' Was Kate imagining it or did those few days sound like a relief? Maybe Mrs Cobb didn't appreciate the house guest.

Kate doubted there was anything sexual between Darcy and Serena. She and Ranjit had done some background checks on Darcy Moss and they weren't altogether surprised that he was single and had never married. Looking at pictures of the young Darcy with some fellow male students, Kate suspected he could be gay but, as a serious Catholic, had supressed his desires and put them in a closet.

When Serena entered, Ranjit took a double take. Kate had told her about Steve Darwin's suggestion to read up about Phyllis Schlafly, the anti-Feminist campaigner who died in 2016. Ranjit decided Schafly was a female version of Donald Trump because she also spoke and wrote passionately against the United Nations, globalization, arms control agreements, free trade, and immigration. He'd seen pictures of her with rigidly styled blond hair and fifties fashion.

The woman walking into the lounge was almost a spitting image in hair style but Serena was taller and considerably less slender. There were pink bows covering the buttons on her cardigan. Kate had told him that she was different to her mentor in some ways. Serena liked posting recipes and household tips. Cakes and 'cookie' baking were favoured. Ranjit agreed that Kate could open the questioning. He wanted to watch Serena Scriver closely.

Kate laid out on the coffee table some press photographs of the protests at the John Radcliffe.

'Can I confirm that this is you?' asked Kate, pointing to Serena holding a placate saying 'Abortion is child murder'.

'Yes, that is me. I know why you are here. I don't hide my opposition to Yasmin Bell and others like her who destroy innocent life but that doesn't mean I wanted her dead.'

'I understand that you are friends with the current Vice President, JD Vance?' said Kate.

'Indeed I am and I encouraged him to write that speech decrying the lack of free speech in this country, given how I have been barred from protesting.'

'I can assure you that you have the right to voice your opinions but at a reasonable distance from patients entering the hospital, to prevent you from harassing them, like you did Dr Yasmin Bell and her patients.'

'Could any of your supporters have wished her dead, Mrs Shriver?'

'My supporters are PRO Life. How dare you suggest that I would encourage murder!'

'Do you support your government's request to Romania to lift the travel ban on the misogynist Andrew Tate?' asked Kate.

'That question has no relevance to this case. I want to end this interview. If you want to talk to me in future, my attorney will be present.'

Ranjit adopted a soothing low key voice.

'I'm sure that won't be necessary, Mrs Shriver. I only have one more question for you.'

'Where were you on Feb 28?'

'I was staying here with Darcy.'

'And in the afternoon?'

Serena took her pink diary out of her pink handbag.

'I went to lunch at The Ivy with Barbara Covet before she headed for Cardiff. She was going to help arrange for me to speak there. I took a taxi back here to write my daily podcast.'

'What time would that be?'

'The booking at the Ivy was at 12.30. The taxi company probably knows what time they picked me up.'

She stood up and left the room.

***

Kate went to find the housekeeper and asked her to tell her employer that they were ready for him. They prepared to face Darcy Moss's smooth impassive expression.

'I do hope you haven't been upsetting my influential guest?'

'I think you understand why we needed to ask her some serious questions. We have to find out who hated Yasmin Bell enough to kill her,' said Kate.

'How is it you know Serena Shriver?' asked Ranjit.

'We first met in the USA at a conference at Yale University in 2019.'

'Are we to assume that you share her views on abortion?

'Yes. I do and have always been a Catholic. We corresponded and when she said her son Gideon was coming here to study theology and politics at Richmond College I invited her to stay. This house is large and she can have a wing to herself.'

'Did you support her protests outside your hospital and the jostling of your colleague Yasmin Bell?' asked Kate.

'We had our differences of opinion but we were civilised about it. She respected my position and I didn't interfere with her clinic.' Ranjit noticed that his eyes softened as he said that.

'That didn't answer my question, Mr Moss. Do you support the harassment of your colleagues?'

'I support free speech.'

'I'm sure you do, but what is your opinion of your guest accusing your colleagues of being murderers?'

'I am not Serena's policeman.'

Ranjit suspected that they wouldn't get a straight answer from him, so asked,

'Does Nurse Barbara Covet share Serena Shriver's views?'

'I have no idea. You'd better ask her.'

***

'What do you think about Mr Darcy Moss, sir?'

'I'm reserving my opinion but I want to talk to Dr Azad. I haven't met him yet. Can you talk to some of Yasmin's other colleagues? Find out more about the Covet Moss– Shriver dynamic.'

'We asked the administrator about Barbara Covet but not about Moss. I think Yasmin could have complained about him, too?'

Chapter 16

The team gathered to share their feedback. Richard Smith the IT expert had news.

'That car checks out, Sir, but I can't be a hundred per cent sure it was Barbara Covet driving. The driver is most probably a woman but, in that woolly hat and scarf, it's hard to be sure. I looked to see if there are cameras near where her parents live. But there are none in her suburb. It's a low crime area.'

'Royal Taxis say they picked up Serena Shriver at 2.15pm,' said Peter Jordan.

'I'm going to group these four together: Serena Shriver, Darcy Moss, Barbara Covet. See what you can find out about the administrator, Chen. Does she meet them outside of work too?'

'Yes Sir. You asked me to research Moss. He does LOTS of private work. I pretended to be a potential patient and rang the clinics where he works. The Burford Clinic said he no longer works there but didn't say why.

'Richard helped me look at their records. I noticed that, around that time, they dismissed a nurse and accused her of *bringing the clinic into disrepute*. I went to see her. Sir, I think she could be a whistle blower being badly treated. There's a rumour that she complained about Moss doing unnecessary surgery.'

'Was that publicised?'

'No Sir. I got the impression that the management are wary of him because he's so well connected. He's an alumni of Christ Church and mixes with high-flying Conservative politicians in All Souls.'

'Well done, Chen. That's useful to know. So far it's just rumours. Let's do some digging and see what we can unearth.'

'So are any of these three capable of doing those injuries to Yasmin?'

'The surgeon and Covet who's helped him at some of his operations?' said Kate.

'I'm not sure Shriver is capable of inflicting those wounds on Yasmin Bell and she wouldn't have had enough time either but we need to investigate her followers. Judging by JD Vance's posts, I don't doubt he has supporters who are capable of that kind of hate.'

'The key is that umbilical cord. Was that the only reason for Yasmin's unease at working with Barbara Covet? Did she feel judged by her as Covet won't assist at abortions?' asked Ranjit.

'Who else could have removed that kind of material and could anyone remove it from hospital waste bins or have contacts with designated companies who dispose of hazardous and human waste?' suggested Peter Jordan.

'Good question. Apart from these three and possibly some of Serena Shriver's supporters, the only other positive lead, is the Revolutionary Guard of Iran and, in that case, the killer could have used that method as a red herring.

Richard Smith interrupted.

'Regarding that, sir – a name came up when we looked at dual national hostages imprisoned by the Iranian State. Do you remember when Nazanin Zaghari-Ratcliffe was released? A Thames Reach resident, Araash Azad was freed soon after her. He'd been arrested nine months earlier while on a business trip. He's a relation of Dr Jim Azad – an older cousin and he lives in Thames Reach not far from Radley Large Wood.'

'Thank you Richard. I've arranged to talk to Jim Azad in the morning and that will be useful. This is one of the most complicated cases I've known. We need every bit of help we can get. We are on the murderer's trail but have a long way to go to identify him or her.'

Ranjit had decided to interview Azad at the lab.

'Can you explain to me what you do here?'

'My PhD is in genetics. I qualified as a doctor but I no longer do surgery or clinics like Yasmin. I concentrate on research and advice on cases that involve genetics.'

'What kind of cases?'

'You may have heard in the news of a baby with a rare condition of the eyes. She was born only distinguishing light and dark. Using gene therapy, Moorfields Eye hospital was able to give the baby some sight. I advise in cases like that.'

'That must be rewarding but my colleague interviewed Mr Darcy Moss and he didn't seem to approve of what you and Yasmin Bell were doing.'

'Mr Moss is against a lot of things.'

'Serena Shriver is staying with him. Has she opinions on what your lab does?'

'You would need to ask her but some of her supporters have demonstrated and preached against what we do.'

'Did Yasmin discuss the opposition with you?'

'She showed me nasty emails calling her a baby killer and that she should watch her back. Given that her main aim was to bring healthy babies into the world, it hurt.'

'Do you know who sent them?'

'The hatemongers are international and on social media. They share names of surgeons who carry out abortions. It never used to be a problem in this country but that's changing.'

'Remind me of the last time you saw Yasmin.'

'I had a meal with her the day before she died and I told your colleague that she phoned me on the day she died, saying she was working from home but would come into the lab around 4pm. She didn't seem to be afraid.'

'What did she talk about over the last meal you had together?'

'She talked about her Mum and the work she did at Asylum Welcome. Most of the Iranian refugees are men and she wondered how to help some female activists to leave Iran.'

'Yasmin had bought a house in Thames Reach. Did you visit her there?'

'I've been to the house but not often, we mostly met in restaurants. There's an Iranian one and a Lebanese one in the Cowley Road which we like...'

Jim stopped mid-sentence.

'I keep thinking Yasmin is going to walk in.'

Ranjit looked Azad in the eye. He looked like he cared but could it be a good act?

'Do you want to take a break?'

Azad shook his head.

'So you don't go to Thames Reach much?'

'No.'

'Not even to see your cousin Akaash?'

Azad appeared uncomfortable.

'We rarely meet. He travels a lot. That was how he came to be a hostage in Iran.'

'Can you let me have his contact details?'

Azad wrote them down and handed them to Ranjit who thanked him and left. He was convinced Azad was hiding something. For some reason he couldn't determine, Ranjit didn't believe that he and his cousin rarely met. As he arrived at his car, his phone rang.

'You'd better get back here pronto, Sir - a delegation from MI5 is waiting for you,' said Peter Jordan.

Chapter 17

Ranjit had seen some MI5 operatives at the MET but only from a distance because he was usually assigned to traffic and 'domestics.' Two agents were waiting in his office. His first words were,

'I hope you've been looked after?'

You could pass Dorothy Mead on the street and not give her a second look. 'Possibly in her late fifties but could be younger than she looks,' thought Ranjit, taking in her Margaret Thatcher-era suit and her mousey permed hair. She was clearly not tempted to colour it. Her glasses looked the cheapest on offer whereas her colleague Thomas Said cared a lot about his trim appearance and his fitness.

'It's not often anyone dressed in a Saville Row suit enters this building,' thought Ranjit. 'Said could be a modern day James Bond. The age of this smooth looking operator? Anything from 38- 50.'

Ranjit was not a happy man. As a detective he needed to assess people quickly but not in a stereotypical manner. He decided to leave it as 'Said works out'. Ranjit didn't need to look at himself to be aware that Jia's delicious Indian cuisine had consequences. Thinking of Jia, an image flashed of his wife colouring a few stray bits of grey. Jia looked ten years younger than her age, not ten years older like Dorothy Mead.

'To what do we owe the pleasure of this visit?'

Dorothy Mead opened the discussion.

'Chief Inspector Singh, I don't doubt that you already know the answer to your question. Inspector Jordan, who looked after us, wasn't in the least surprised to see us. He volunteered that you'd considered consulting us.'

Ranjit wasn't sure how to react to that but said,

'That's correct. There are two international aspects to the murder of Dr Bell but I thought we should try to rule out any personal enemies before bringing you in.'

'Have you done that?'

'Not completely. It's still early days but there are none of the usual suspects... jealous boyfriends, financial problems, gangs or drugs.'

'We are interested in both the leads in your investigation and three people in particular, Gideon Shriver and Jim and Akaash Azad.'

Ranjit wasn't surprised by the last two but the first made him feel undermined. He hadn't interviewed Serena's son. Why had he overlooked him?

Thomas Said noticed his reaction.

'We are impressed by how quickly you have honed in on these two investigations.'

But Dorothy Mead looked like she wanted to threaten to take over the investigation.

'On the phone, I told Inspector Jordan to show you our files and I see he did that. You're aware of the nature of the attack on the doctor?'

Ranjit spent thirty minutes going through what they knew so far. The coldness and lack of comment of Mead unsettled him. He relaxed a bit when Said described how Iran operates internationally.

'You'll be surprised by how extensive their network is in the UK. It's understandable that you may not have noticed because they mostly target exiled Iranian activists and journalists. Ten years ago, Nazreen Bell was threatened. We caught the criminal they'd paid to carry out the execution when he was surveying her house. He's been useful to us.'

'Why didn't she tell us?'

'Nazreen adapted, stayed active but not so vocal and, to our knowledge, is not in danger. From your notes, she did tell you that the regime keeps an eye on her. I expect she doesn't want to think her daughter's death is anything to do with her activities.'

'Thank you, Mr Said. I appreciate that. I've made a point of reading Interpol files related to Iran and learned that a criminal gang in Sweden, called Foxtrot, has been used by Iran in contract killings. In your experience have they infiltrated any gangs in the Thames Valley?'

Mead stopped the conversation, saying,

'So you understand why we require detailed reporting on BOTH strands of the investigation and there may come a point when we have to take over.'

'You haven't interviewed the parents in depth and I'd like to be present when you do.'

'Early this morning, we gave permission to release the body. Nasreen is Muslim and they want to bury her daughter quickly. I expect that will be Monday. Can the interview wait until Tuesday afternoon?'

'We will return on Tuesday. I also want to be present when you interview Gideon Shriver.'

'Can you help me here? On what grounds should I interview him? He was present at a demonstration at the JR but that is all we know.'

'Let's just say he's an ambitious man and his mother is ambitious for him too.'

After reporting on the day's events to the Chief Constable, Ranjit asked Richard Smith, their civilian IT expert, to get as much information as possible on Gideon Shriver. Ranjit left for the weekend feeling utterly drained, leaving Peter Jordan and Veronica Chen in charge.

Home was filled with teenagers and a mixture of Taylor Swift and Bhangra assaulted his ears. It was a relief. When he'd uprooted his family from West London to Oxford, the twins were devastated as they had to leave their friends behind. Two years later they were both thriving but in different ways.

Since their trip to Amritsar, Roshan had become religious and was keen to explore his Sikh heritage. On Saturday evenings, he joined a band of local Sikhs of all ages, feeding the homeless. He had bonded with two Sikh boys at Cheney School. They were often in his room with rhythmic Bhangra in the background but Ranjit suspected they were probably playing computer games.

In contrast, nearly all of Amber's friends were white and were devotees of Taylor Swift. Jia was in the kitchen cooking. Ranjit gave her a kiss and asked how her day had been.

'It's not good news. Brookes has announced its going to close its Music and Maths departments – can you believe that?'

'Your post is secure though?' Jia was an administrator in the nursing department.

'For the moment but Cardiff is closing its nursing course. What a mad world we live in! Given the chronic shortage of nurses, we have to poach staff from the poorest countries, and yet they want to close nursing courses!

'Enough about me. What about your week? You left at 6.30 and mostly arrived home after ten when I was ready to switch off. We haven't talked at all.'

'I'm not sure that I even want to talk about it, honey. Once this case is over, I'll need to put it behind me and bury it deep in my subconscious. By the look of it, the twins won't want to talk to their old dad today.'

'It's butter chicken, chilli paneer and fried rice tonight. It'll be ready in half an hour. Why don't you get yourself a beer and chill out – watch the football?'

Ranjit felt like he was a lucky man.

***

Meanwhile in Thames Reach, Steve Darwin had booked a taxi to take himself and Alex Hornby to Gino's for an Italian meal before going to a comedy show at the Old Fire Station. Steve was fifteen years older than Alex but they'd discovered they enjoyed each other's company. He for one wanted more.

Over their spaghetti, he regaled Alex with tales of his friend Gavin McGeorge.

'You know they call him Dr Bug because he dresses up like a stag beetle and gets on stilts to talk to children about his passion for insects. Did you see him crawl out of that log in that TV series from South America? He was covered from head to toe in termites but said "I've never had such a good time in a log before!"

He raised his glass and leant in towards Alex.

'This is more like my idea of a good time.'

But Alex was mulling over the name Dr Bug.

'What's in a name? Here's to all beetle lovers. George Gamble is interested in insects too, particularly butterflies. At lunch on Sunday, don't ask him about them, or his meal will go cold. Usually he's a man of few words but mention flora and fauna, and it's like pressing a start button.'

Chapter 18

It was almost lunch time on Sunday. Kate and George waved to each other as they approached Alex's house from opposite directions and were both on the doorstep when Alex opened the door. They were surprised to see Steve sitting comfortably in the living room looking very much at home. Kate couldn't help it: she observed Alex and Steve's body language. George took off his boots.

'Sorry, I've been in Bagley Wood and saw my first brimstone of the year and even caught sight of a grass snake coming out of hibernation.'

'Where was that?' asked Alex.

George was slow to answer, because it had been at Chandling's lake.

'They like to head for the water once they emerge from hibernation. Spring is springing.'

'At least you don't have poisonous reptiles in England,' said Steve and started telling rattle snake stories.

'We have adders but they are shy creatures and rarely bite a human being,' said George.

'The only dangerous reptiles around here are human. They certainly know how to kill in a way you'll never forget,' said Alex.

'F**k, that's poisoned the atmosphere. I'm sorry but I haven't been able to walk in that direction since finding Yasmin. I don't think I can ever go there again, not even to help harmless amphibians and look for grass snakes.'

'Snake in the grass? That's a good description of who we are looking for,' said Kate.

'Excuse me a minute...' Alex headed for the kitchen looking tearful.

'We need to change the subject,' said Steve.

'While Alex is in the kitchen, do you know Gideon Shriver? We have to interview him next week,' asked Kate.

'I've not met him but have seen him on TV often enough, mostly with his mother. He's building a following on social media. His mother is grooming him to stand as Republican for Congress despite only being twenty three.'

'What kind of following does he have?'

'Disaffected boys, mostly Incels.'

George wondered what kind of animals were 'incels' but understood soon enough.

'Is he involuntarily celibate?' asked Kate.

'Make up your own mind when you meet him. He's never been that far from his mother and she doesn't believe in sex before marriage.'

Over a long slow Caribbean meal washed down with generous glasses of wine the atmosphere changed. Alex put on some reggae and everyone chilled. George and Kate eyed each other and nodded. They gave Alex a hug, thanked her for the meal and left Steve and Alex to what Kate suspected could be an amorous afternoon.

Chapter 19

Ranjit had relaxed over the weekend and felt able to joke with Kate.

'Jia persuaded me to watch a Bollywood movie at the Vue on Sunday. I realised that there's another man in our marriage – Shah Rukh Khan.'

Kate looked confused.

'He's the top paid Bollywood film star. I can't compete.'

Kate looked surprised but pleased. This was the first time in the nearly three years she'd known Ranjit that he'd been relaxed enough to joke with her.

'Maybe I can lure him away, Sir?'

But she immediately regretted the repartee. In her police career she'd often been marginalised by unwanted sexist jokes and didn't want to play into that culture.

'Ignore that, please, Sir. Given that we are going to interview Gideon Shriver I've been doing some digging.'

'Anything interesting?'

'He's an Incel, sir, with a growing following of disaffected young men.'

'Could that be why the intelligence services are interested in him, do you think?'

'That combined with his political ambitions. His mother is keen for him to stand for Congress and given what's happening in American politics he's in with a chance to grow support in the Republican Party. His mother is influential in the mould of her heroine, Phyllis Shaffley.'

'Thanks a lot. Good work. So he's the kind who boasts of calling a spade a spade.'

'Calling a spade a fork more like ....'

The Inspector's phone rang. He moved away from DS Farr and, when he returned, he looked cheerful.

'That was Dorothy Mead. The good news is that she won't be coming to Richmond College to interview Gideon Shriver. She's confirmed what you just told me and has contacted Gideon's tutor, Rev Dr Philip Parks. She says we must see him too and mention her name. He will then talk freely to us. She wants to know who Gideon is mixing with, the theme of his thesis and whether he's writing his thesis himself or using AI to do it for him.'

'So not much then,' grinned Kate.

***

The lodge let Gideon know they'd arrived. He came with his tutor, so Ranjit said,

'We'd like to interview Mr Shriver alone, please, but we can have a few words with you before we leave?'

'You can use my room and give me a text when you have finished.'

Kate's mother had worked for a while for an antiques business and her daughter had also acquired a discerning eye. Kate quickly summed up Rev Park's room. It was lined with books and the shelves looked early Edwardian. The office was dominated by a late Victorian mahogany partners' desk and an upholstered swivel chair, a grandfather clock and a chesterfield settee. If it wasn't for the computer, it could have been a pre-First World War Don's study.

Ranjit took the tutor's chair and Gideon sat in the hard chair on the other side of the desk. Kate stood behind him.

'I'm sorry to take up your time but, as you know, a young doctor was killed not far from where your mother is staying in Boar's Hill. Mr Moss told us that you sometimes stay there and indeed you were there on the night she was killed.'

'Mr Moss told us the sad news. Yasmin Bell worked under him and her parents live not far from his house but Darcy says he hasn't met them. I don't see how I can help you.'

'It's a routine question. Where were you on the afternoon and evening of February 28?'

Gideon put on a pair of Gucci glasses and said,

'Let me look in my diary.'

He looked at the calendar on his phone and replied,

'I was here in the morning. I attended a lecture by Dr Parks. After lunch in college, at some point in the afternoon – I can't remember what time, I cycled to Boars Hill. I stayed there over-night.'

'Thank you. There's a reason why we need to try and eliminate you from our enquiries. It is because of the circumstances in which you met Dr Bell.'

Ranjit took out a photo taken at the demonstration at the JR where Gideon was holding a poster accusing her of being a murderer.

'What have you to say about this?'

Gideon began to reply in a soft modulated Southern USA voice but from behind, Kate noticed his fist clench under the desk.

'The UK claims to be a free country with freedom of speech and I am entitled to my opinions. I am upholding the word of God.'

'You have the right to your opinion and to voice it but, in this country, you do not have the right to threaten people going about their lawful business,' said Ranjit, stressing the NOT.

'There is man's law and God's law and I am on the side of God's law.'

'There are many interpretations of that, Mr Shriver. To most people in this country your protest appears to threaten the health and wellbeing of valued health workers. Dr Bell certainly told her colleagues that she felt intimidated. Now that she is dead, we have to ask whether you incited that violence and who had a reason to kill her.'

'Detective Singh, this interview has come to an end. You have your work to do and I have mine.'

Gideon held out his hand to shake, but Ranjit ignored it.

'We'll need to talk more. If you are unwilling, then it will have to be at the station. For the moment we can leave it here.'

Gideon left the room and Kate rang Rev Parks to say the interview had come to an abrupt end.

***

Ranjit asked him if he would like his chair but he sat on the one vacated by Gideon.

'I understand Mr Shriver is writing a DPhil. What's the subject of his thesis?'

'He is exploring a "biblical model" for women to pursue in romantic relationships with a partner who is "protector and a leader".'

'What do you think about that?'

'I am encouraging him to explore a variety of examples of relationships not just a patriarchal model.'

'I believe you had a call from Dorothy Mead?'

'Yes, but I'm not sure how much help I can be.'

'What do you think of Gideon's academic ability?

'Not much frankly. I suspect he's using AI. I insist he do some work under my supervision but he's an adult and I can't treat him like a child.'

'I believe it was his mother's idea that he come here. Is Serena Shriver giving the college a large donation?'

'I can't deny that. Richmond College is not a wealthy institution.'

'What can you tell us of Gideon's activities outside of his studies? Is he in a relationship?'

'Not that I know of. I feel somewhat sorry for him. His mother has a strong personality and doesn't believe in sex before marriage. To me, he's a frustrated young man who spends far too much time on his phone. If you have the means to see what he's watching, that could be useful.'

'Is there anything else you think we should know?'

'I suspect the reason Dorothy's showing an interest is his politics. In the last US election, his mother was a key supporter of the Vice President, JD Vance. We all know he's been saying unfriendly things about the UK, EU and Ukraine.'

Kate couldn't hold back.

'Yea, he wanted Zelensky to wear a suit even though his country is at war. Maybe even an expensive Gucci like those specs Gideon was wearing?'

Philip Park allowed himself a wry smile.

'Serena wants her son to have an Oxford degree to give him gravitas. She likes the idea of Dr Gideon Shriver. Up to a point she supports Trump but she isn't keen on his style. He's an old man and she is thinking long term. She's building her son's reputation in the Republican Party. Given the state of US politics, you may have just interviewed a future President.'

'Thank you for your help.'

***

On the ten minute drive back to police headquarters in Kidlington, Kate observed:

'Sir, we both know that Dr Moss would be capable of doing

the crime but I can't see a strong enough motive. He may be against abortions, but he doesn't seem to be an ideologue. Gideon is different. He gave me the creeps, Sir.'

'I have an ambitious daughter. Amber is considering medicine as a career. I'm finding his misogynist propaganda disturbing. What do you think of our potential President of the USA?' asked Ranjit, emphasising the YOU.

'His name is prophetic. It sounds like he wants to create a kind of Gilead – the dystopian vision that Margaret Atwood created in *A Handmaid's Tale*.'

'What's that about?' asked Ranjit, who wasn't much of reader.

Kate did her best to explain but when she mentioned the TV series, he got it.

'It's the one with women wearing weird red gowns and bonnets. Jia watched that.'

'Now we have to prepare for the meeting with Akaash tomorrow. This is the most difficult case I've known with its undertones of the worst international politics.'

Kate thought Ranjit was about to say *I'm out of my depth.* When he didn't, she queried,

'Had we better ring Said when we get back to the station?

'Good idea. I can do that and I'll let you know in the morning. Why don't you get home early for once? The dilemmas will still be here in the morning.'

Chapter 20

It was only 6 o'clock when Kate arrived in Thames Reach so she gave Alex a ring and asked if she'd like to go out for supper 'on me.'

'Can Steve come and we go Dutch?

'Alex! Are you a twosome?'

'Joined at the hip,' laughed Alex.

Kate was delighted. Finding Yasmin's body had changed her friend. Some joy was blossoming again, thanks to Steve. There was a large age difference – fifteen years between them but he was such an interesting guy that Kate understood the attraction.

'Shall we try The Fox on Boars Hill? It's got new management.'

Kate sensed a shiver over the airwaves at the mention of Boars Hill.

Alex took a deep breath.

'Why not? Do we need to book?'

***

Alex felt at ease when she saw her artist friend Diana with her husband at a nearby table. She introduced them to Steve and Kate before their food arrived.

'I've enjoyed walks with Diana. She collects bark of different textures to use in collages. I sometimes envy her - her art is inspired by nature and not like mine by crime.'

'Given how interested you are in history, I've often wondered why crime and not historical fiction, Alex?'

'Good question. I need to earn a living. Teaching creative writing and crime pays! There's a gap in the summer and that's when I take in foreign students.'

'I get it, creativity doesn't pay these days. The money's in the tech not the content,' said Steve. Then he glanced at Kate.

'What inspired you to join the police?'

'A boy in my class was a victim of knife crime. The police officers who came into the school impressed me. At a careers conference, I learned about a scheme where the MET paid your university fees if you guaranteed to join the force after graduating. That appealed to me. No loans to repay!'

'Is it in order to ask about your day?'

'Not in detail but as you know about the case and I trust you both not to talk about it to my boss or your friends, I'll make an exception.'

Kate described the visit to Richmond College.

'Rev Parks looked positively reptilian… toad-like. Sorry Alex, that's insensitive of me, reminding you…'

Alex decided to change the tone.

'Kate, do you really want to trash my reputation with the Friends of Radley Large Wood? You do realise we have experts on all forms of wildlife and toads are NOT reptiles, they're amphibians!'

Kate looked relieved.

'That means Gideon Shriver fits the description better. He tries to appear as smooth as silk. In my imagination, he resembled a snake whose head is slightly raised, tongue tasting the air ready to strike. But, in our case he recoiled – ducked out.'

'Snake-like is a good description of that reactionary movement,' said Steve.

'They insinuate themselves deep in the culture of my country and distort it.'

Alex looked approvingly at Steve.

'Coming from an Afro-Caribbean background, the church

played a big role in my life growing up. I often think that, if Jesus turned up at Serena's church in South Carolina, they'd turn him away because he looked like a Palestinian and not white like them.'

Steve nodded in approval.

'Alex and Steve really are getting close' thought Kate. Steve interrupted her inner smile.

'I went to the Ashmolean to see the Anselm Keifer exhibition. He portrayed visually how the Nazis did that – how they subverted German Culture. He used snakes to ensnare portraits of Arminius, Brunhilde, Kant and Nietzsche. The likes of Gideon and his mother want us to believe that they are the people of the Bible but ignore that Jesus told the story of the Good Samaritan and befriended the outcasts of society.'

'Gosh we are having a deep conversation tonight but thank you because this case seems to have links to so much that is happening in the world. Tomorrow, we move from American reptiles to Iranian ones. Most murders are solved in the first weeks and there's forensic evidence to help prove it. This is such a complicated and difficult case. We are doing everything we can to find out who did it, Alex,' said Kate.

'That's Oxford for you – *all the world connects here*. There's hardly any period of British history when Oxford hasn't played a significant role and its influence ripples across the continents,' stated Alex.

'You are spot on. The effects of Empire are still being felt and yet it doesn't look to me that many young British people know much about it. You should tackle it in a young adult book, Alex,' said Steve.

'I'm beginning to feel under pressure,' laughed Alex as she raised a glass to her friends. 'But, maybe you're right. I shouldn't underestimate myself. Come to think of it, St Hilda's underestimated Thames Reach. They hadn't anticipated the depth of expertise in our village when it comes to bats, badgers, amphibians and reptiles! At least, in the UK, there's only one poisonous snake: the really venomous ones are foreign!'

Chapter 21

'Do you still want me to be the family liaison officer with the Bells, Sir? I'm feeling guilty because we haven't kept them in the loop. I'm not sure what to tell them. They've buried her and have organised a memorial service for her tomorrow in Worcester College Chapel. That's where Jonathan Bell is a fellow. Yasmin trained in London at UCL.'

'Yes, you should see them today but I'd also like you with me for the interview with Akaash Azad. Let's go together after that. Give them a ring and see if 4pm is okay?'

'I've asked Chen and Richard Smith to dig into Serena Shriver and Gideon's activities and Peter Jordan to find out more about Barbara Covet and her Mr Moss. But now, we must collect our secret service *colleague* from the station, he's coming with us to Akaash.' Ranjit's stress on the word 'colleague' did not sound convincing.

'What do you think of Thomas Said?'

'He's a smooth one, Sir.'

***

On the fifteen minute drive to Thames Reach, Said asked them how much they knew about recent events in Iran. Kate replied,

'I watched the Women, Life, Freedom protests in response to the death of Mahsa Amini in custody of Iran's morality police. We're aware that Yasmin helped a fellow doctor who had taken part in the uprising.'

'Those protests involved young men and women throughout Iran but their demands for change were met with a brutal crackdown. We are talking hundreds of deaths and tens of thousands of arbitrary arrests. If the government of Iran wanted to get rid of Yasmin Bell, they'd have no qualms.'

'The Islamic State Group boast about their crimes. Isn't it similar with Iran's Revolutionary Guard? Have you heard anything?' asked Ranjit.

'They haven't claimed responsibility. They don't always. The bizarre mutilations would make sense is if they don't want us to think it is them. There was a case in New York where the criminal told the hit man they needed to *overkill* to send a message – they decapitated the man.'

'Do you think that could that be the motive in this case?' asked Ranjit.

'Foreign relations are currently their utmost priority and not internal opposition. But we can't rule them out. What is certain is that, if they are responsible, they would have employed a criminal to do it. In our interview, I'm most interested in recent visitors to Akaash Azad. Let's conduct this interview as if he is a victim of the Iranian State and in no way a suspect.'

'Is he a suspect?' asked Ranjit.

'He was released early with no signs of torture. That doesn't mean he wasn't tortured and is indeed innocent. I have my reasons to be suspicious that he was released early having been persuaded to help them. He may have been unwilling but afraid. Not everyone is as courageous as Yasmin's mother.'

***

Akaash showed them into his conservatory. Kate realised that the view from his window had transformed in the last few months. Where he had once looked out on beautiful woodland, beyond a low hedge at the bottom of his garden she saw a sea of mud. Kate couldn't help whispering the lyrics of the Flanders and Swann's hippopotamus song – *Glorious Mud.* Her father loved their wit and had often sung their compositions. 'But...' thought Kate, 'it may be paradise for hippos but not for lovers of Radley Large Wood.'

'You were saying?' queried Ranjit.

'Sorry, thinking aloud, Sir.'

Ranjit opened the interview,

'We're following up on all contacts of Yasmin Bell. As your cousin was such a good friend of hers and you live in Thames Reach, we assume you knew her.'

'Not really. We met recently but not through Jim. We were on a protest walk about that.' He pointed to the quagmire. 'Residents around here are upset about the way the wood is being managed. Its owners, St Hilda's College, claim that is what they are doing, '*managing*' it. In just three months they've cut down a great chunk of this ancient woodland to replant it. Strange isn't it? You can get money for planting new trees but not for looking after old ones.'

Kate looked sympathetic but changed the subject.

'Why didn't Jim introduce you?'

'We may be cousins but we don't meet often.'

'Don't you get on?'

'We get on fine, when we meet. How often do you get to-gether with your cousins?'

'In my case, they don't live just three miles away.'

Said interrupted:

'How are you Akaash? You'll remember me. I did your debrief-ing when you were released.'

'Thank you, yes. You helped a lot. I enjoyed your jokes about my name.'

He turned to the others.

'Azaad means *freedom* which is ironic if you're banged up in Evin Prison. The Ayatollahs are willing to take anyone hostage if they think they can trade them. As you are here, does that mean you suspect Iranian involvement in Yasmin's death?'

'That's one theory,' said Ranjit.

'Jim hasn't discussed the possibility with you?'

'No, I haven't seen him since her death.'

'You haven't rung him or written to him with condolences?'

'I've been meaning to but haven't got round to it. I'm going to the memorial service tomorrow and intend to talk to him there.'

Said intervened again.

'Do you know if Jim or any of your Iranian acquaintances have had any visitors from Iran in recent months?'

'Not that I know of,' said Akaash, avoiding eye contact.

'And yourself? Have you felt threatened?'

'Unlike Yasmin and Nasreen, I've kept a low profile. As long as I'm not active opposing them and I don't visit Iran, I'm safe. I feel bad about it but I want a quiet life.'

Ranjit asked where he was on the day of Yasmin's murder. And he handed them a programme of the conference he attended that day in Oxford at Green Templeton College, so his alibi could easily be checked.

'Thomas knows that I'm a chemist and work for Smith Collins, the pharmaceutical company. I was on a sales drive in Tehran when they arrested me.'

'Thanks for your help. We'll be at the memorial tomorrow. So if we need to ask you any more questions, we can see you briefly afterwards.'

***

'Well, he's lying,' concluded Thomas Said.

Chapter 22

'How can you be so sure that he's lying?' asked Ranjit.

'He's had several visitors from Tehran in recent months and one stayed the night with him.'

'How do you know that? Have you their identities?'

'One of them works for us. Let me check them out and if it looks relevant to the case, I promise I'll share the information with you. Can you drop me at All Souls, please? I have a meeting there.'

After dropping him off, Ranjit turned to Kate.

'Thomas Said moves in exalted circles. Not like us run of the mill cops.'

Kate replied,

'Speak for yourself. You don't know who I mix with in my time off.'

'That famous American, Steve Darwin?'

'Alex Hornby has bagged him. He's divorced and I wonder what his son will make of her when he comes with his family at Easter.'

***

Spring had come to Boar's Hill. Daffodils swayed in a light breeze and the birds were in full-throated song. Dog walkers on the old golf course were relishing the view of the dreaming spires of Oxford. Kate and Ranjit approached the Bells' house with the opposite feeling–reluctance. They were shown into the lounge. Sorrow was etched on Jonathan and Nasreen's faces and their eyes were dimmed by timeless loss.

'We won't take up much of your time. You will want to concentrate on tomorrow's memorial. We'll be there to show our respects. May I ask why the college chapel, since I presume Yasmin was not a Christian?'

'We gave her a Muslim burial. Although she was culturally Muslim, Yasmin didn't have a religious mind-set. I don't like labels. She took the best from my culturally Christian background and from Nasreen's Muslim heritage and stirred science into the mix.'

Nasreen nodded her agreement.

'Worcester is Jonathan's college and the chapel is a jewel: a colourful setting for her not religious memorial. The college is doing the catering too. Our job was to find a place large enough but intimate enough for everyone who wants to remember Yasmin...'

Nasreen choked as she spoke her daughter's name.

'Excuse me...' and she left the room in distress.

'We are so sorry to intrude on your grief, Sir.'

'You have a job to do and I would like to know more...'

'I wish we could tell you that we know who killed your daughter. This is such a difficult and complicated case. We can find no evidence to point to a personal or financial motive for this crime. Today we have been investigating links to Iran. If you have any information related to that, it will be much appreciated.'

Jonathan confirmed Said's account of events in 2015.

'That's when we installed those,' pointing to the security gates.

'If it's a political murder carried out by the Revolutionary Guard, you won't bring them to justice. Whoever did it would have left the country immediately afterwards. Think Russia and the Salisbury poisonings. The murderers were out of the country within twenty four hours of committing that crime.'

'At least those murderers were named but, you're right, they've not had to face justice.'

Nasreen came back in the room and through tears said,

'I can't believe she has gone. She was so full of vitality. With both medicine and research, she worked long hours but still found time for exercise, being there for her friends and for us. If you are coming to the memorial, you'll hear accounts of her courage and intelligence. As her mother I am biased but her death is a huge loss of potential. She had so much to give.'

'Will Darcy Moss be at the memorial?'

'I expect so. It wouldn't look good if he doesn't attend.'

Kate noticed an edge to Nasreen's voice.

'I don't think she likes him,' thought Kate but Ranjit said,

'He is a scientist too but talks about being a practising Catholic. And that appears to influence him?'

'I see where you are going, Inspector. Do you suspect her murderer was related to her work?' asked Nasreen.

There was an edge of hope in the way she said 'work'.

Chapter 23

Ranjit didn't know much about architecture and regretted it as soon as he walked into Worcester College Chapel. He recognised that it was different to the Gothic chapels in most colleges. The brochure produced by the family had a footnote about the building. He read that it had been repainted in 1863. Every inch was colourful. He noticed Kate run a finger over a dodo carved at the end of the stall where they were sitting. There were other carved animals, real and mythological including a unicorn. In Amber's primary school there'd been a craze for them. His eyes rested on the mosaic floor. Every surface was a delight. Where a coffin would usually be placed was a vibrant Persian carpet and a huge inlaid vase overflowing with multihued flowers.

The pews were filling up. Kate saw George and Alex, Samantha and Steve enter and sit in the opposite pews to them. Ranjit's attention was on the brochure and the photographs of Yasmin including one of her with her Iranian grandmother. They were looking at each other with affection in the way Roshan looked at his grandmother. It made this memorial feel personal.

He saw the organ near the entrance but no organist. Strains of recorded music grew gradually louder: the Festival of Baghdad. Another one of those historical complications. After Saddam Hussein's overthrow, the schisms his brutal rule had kept at bay erupted like a volcano. If Iran was anything to do with Yasmin's death, they could have employed an Iraqi Shiite criminal just as easily as an Iranian one. Ranjit ran a hand over his eyes. He didn't want to go down that road. He saw Thomas Said enter with the Vice Chancellor of Oxford University. Said must have stayed in All Souls overnight. Unusually for a Vice Chancellor, Irene Tracey had attended a state school close to their Police Headquarters in

Kidlington... unlike Yasmin Bell who went to Oxford High School.

Some key dates were interspersed with photographs on the Memorial Service Programme. Ranjit read it through to see if there was anything he didn't know.

Dr Yasmin Bell

December 29, 1991: Born to Nasreen and Jonathan Bell in Kingston on Thames.

1994- 1998: In Syria where Jonathan had a diplomatic posting. Here were the lovely pictures of her in Shiraz with her grandmother.

2002: Family moved to Boars Hill

2009: He read about the gap year Yasmin spent with Mariam Thompson, the actress who played a minor role in the Harry Potter series. Yasmin and Mariam had spent some of their gap year volunteering for a charity called the Nasio Trust in west Kenya before exploring East Africa and the USA. (Pictures of the two at the Equator and in Washington DC in an open-topped red car).

'The 5 foot 4 inch Yasmin with her brown curly hair, lightly tanned skin and large dark eyes sitting contrasted with the tall slender Mariam with her straight blonde hair and dark sunglasses,' thought Ranjit. 'They would have met at Oxford High. Mariam's career had been growing ever since. Then the hard work for Yasmin,'

September 2010: Yasmin studied medicine at University College London. Proud graduation pictures outside the Royal Albert Hall.

September 2017: Registrar at John Radcliffe Maternity Hospital.

2019: Studied for her D Phil at Green Templeton College

Oxford under Professor Baldwin. (Pic in her doctorial robe at the Sheldonian.)
2022: Combined University of Oxford post of Researcher at Nuffield Price Laboratory and senior registrar at the JR.
2023: Bought house in Thames Reach. (House warming party photograph)

Ranjit noticed not just Jim, but also his cousin in that photo.
Followed by a list of publications and citations relating to Gene Editing in Infants. (A selection of publications including the Lancet)
Died February 28, 2025
The College chaplain asked them to stand and sing the hymn, *Love Divine, All Love's Excelling* but that was to be one of few gestures of a religious rite. Jim Azad walked slowly to the lectern to read a poem by Rumi: one of Yasmin's favourites. That was followed by the first tribute by her school friend Mariam.

The girl she described was hard working, enthusiastic and curious. Yasmin was a dedicated learner but was sociable and enjoyed a good time. She described how they dressed up as Spice Girls and walked through Jericho imitating their accents and mannerisms. When she mentioned the two primary schoolgirls had asked for their autographs, the congregation laughed. It felt cathartic. Mariam said Yasmin would like that response.

'Yasmin was never a killjoy and I believe that she would like to be remembered as someone who enhanced our enjoyment of life. She could be fun to be with but was a serious person. Our gap year experience working for the Nasio Trust in Musanda confirmed her desire to become a doctor, her compassion and determination to do something to reduce suffering.'

A slight tremble in Mariam's voice:

'Yasmin was friend in good times and in bad. I can't count the occasions when she came to my aid. When my mother died, I was inconsolable. It was Yasmin who helped me. She said I should talk to my mother. As long as she is in my thoughts she will be alive to me and part of my life. I took her advice and started a scrap book of important events and wrote on the cover, 'For my mother, Joan Thompson.' What I never thought would happen is that I would need to remember the best friend anyone could have ...' She broke down and left the lectern.

As Mariam walked back to her seat, over the sound system came the voice of Dame Kiri Te Tanawa singing Mozart's Dove Sono from the Marriage of Figaro. Ranjit felt the sorrow and regret in the aria. Yasmin's friends and colleagues were visibly moved.

The next tribute was from her PhD Tutor, Professor Baldwin, who told the story of a brilliant mind and a passion for her subject. And she was proving herself as a capable researcher. She wanted to develop that side of her career but her experience in medicine was proving useful in practice with patients. He described the advances she was part of and regretted the loss to science caused by her death.

Two female friends of Iranian ancestry came to the front. One was carrying a tar, a Persian lute. She began to play and then her friend began to sing, in Farsi, a heart breaking song of loss. Jonathan rose to pay tribute to his daughter.

'Yasmin's mother, Nasreen, asked that you come here dressed in bright clothes to celebrate our daughter. Thank you for doing that. You will know that Nasreen and Yasmin have both opposed the dress code enforced on women in Iran. When Nasreen was a child in Iran, her mother wore embroidered traditional Persian clothes and her hair was tied back in a silk scarf but was loose at the back. Nasreen saw colour drained away and it broke her heart.

'When we were posted to Syria, it was too dangerous for Nasreen to cross the border but her mother was able to visit us and we didn't feel we were taking risks letting Yasmin get to know Iran. We wanted Yasmin to love the culture of Iran, the perfumes, the food, music and dance, the poetry, the family picnics, the sensual Persian culture not the joyless version of the Ayatollahs. All the things that Yasmin and Nasreen love are forbidden. That is why today, we want you to remember our beloved daughter with all your senses. The flowers in the chapel are not just colourful like the painted walls and ceiling but are scented too. The food we will serve will be delicious and aromatic. You have listened to beautiful music from different cultures. And you can run your fingers over the carved animals on the pews. Yasmin delighted in using all her senses especially in nature. One of the delights of Boar's Hill and Thames Reach, for her, was running and walking in the woods and by the river listening to birdsong as well as taking in carpets of bluebells and wood anemones in Radley Large Wood.'

He glanced at the floral Persian carpet in front of him.

'While still a schoolgirl she would be excited by glimpses of deer, rabbits and foxes, jumping over molehills and loved scavenger hunting in the woods. That's why she appreciated this song written by Iffley resident, Peggy Seeger. She believed that we share one world and should care for it and for each other. She has been taken so cruelly from us. No parent should experience what we have ... Listen to Peggy's song and, when in nature, please remember our Yasmin. We will try to feel her walking with us on Boar's Hill.'

The lyricist was in the congregation, but they watched on a screen as a younger Peggy sang ...

Slowly slowly she turns over in the night
Turns her lovely face towards the morning light
Always turning turning turning
On her long and endless journey through the skies

Slowly slowly she turns over through the day
Flowers bloom and seed and die and fade away
Seasons turning turning turning
'Til tomorrow's just a memory of today

Virgin water tumbling tumbling down the hill
First the storm and then the time when all is still
All will follow follow follow
All in balance when the earth does as she will

Who invades the sky to bring the goddess down
Who's laid poison in her body in her bones
The earth is trembling trembling trembling
Is she waiting for the deadly final wound

Won't man beware the power of the tide
Learn to answer to the mother's warning cry
Learn to follow follow follow.

Learn to live with all on earth or all will die.

***

Yasmin's mother was last to speak.

'The Assad regime in Syria were allies of Iran. After the Gulf War, we had to leave the Middle East and came to Oxford. Until now, we had not regretted it. Yasmin thrived at Oxford High

School and, when she read for her D Phil, her inspirational tutor, Professor Baldwin, instilled in her a love of research. Jonathan has described how she loved her surroundings. Going through Yasmin's things, we found this poem. We have no idea when she found the time to write it but it's testament to her energy, sensitivity and creativity. It's inspired by the landscape around Boars Hill and Thames Reach and was intended for an anthology to be published on behalf of the Friends of Radley Large Wood. I'd like you to hear Yasmin's words not mine.

The Sound of Silence by Yasmin Bell

Hear the stream trickle down to the city
to wash the stone spires.
Watch the kites circle, in silence, ignore
the inky crow on his tree tower.
Listen to his little cousins' full throated chorus
Great tit, blackbird, thrush, robin and wren.

Touch the bark pictures, hug the trees.
Avoid the woody layers which deceive!
Not oak but bracket fungus.
Smell the hidden universe beneath your feet
Fly agaric, shaggy inkcap, dead man's fingers
The visible apps of the woodland internet.

Seasonal scents of pine, bluebells,
wild rose, honeysuckle and wet leaves.
Smell but don't taste the deadly hemlock and foxgloves.
Sleep beneath the sweet peas by the garden fence.
Savour the taste of blackberry, wild cherry and garlic.
See the sky dipped with dyes and dotted with wisps of clouds.

After that poem – inspired, Kate assumed, by the ongoing work in Radley Large Wood, the music which played them out was Elton John's 'Candle in the Wind.'

Kate had never attended such a poignant memorial. She tried, as a police officer to be detached at events like these but today, she'd failed miserably. Neither had Ranjit expected to feel so moved. Sorrow for Yasmin's parents for their loss of this beautiful spirit, permeated his whole being. He couldn't put the clock back and prevent the evil done to this family but he would do whatever he could to help them. Kate noticed his moist eyes and respected him for it. She recognised something in him that he hadn't revealed to her before, compassion.

The mourners moved at a slow pace out of the chapel to the dining hall where a buffet of Persian and Middle Eastern food was served. Ranjit and Kate were almost the last to leave the chapel. Mariam approached them as they emerged in the cloister.

'Can I talk to you?'

'Of course.'

'Shall we go and sit by the lake? We can talk without being overheard there.'

It was a peaceful spot but Kate couldn't help thinking how it compared to Chandlings with its beautiful pond defiled by the memory of seeing Yasmin's damaged body. That was not the first time she had seen hate turn beauty into ugliness.

'Yasmin's parents will appreciate your words just now. That was a lovely tribute to your friend.'

'It was all true. A light has gone out. Elton John's song is right for Yasmin. I wanted to ask you if you were aware that her consultant boss, Mr Moss did not attend the memorial?'

'Yes we did take note of that. As well as paying our respects to the family, we are taught to observe who attends funerals and see if their behaviour gives rise to suspicions.'

'In December, I was working in LA and Yasmin gave me a WhatsApp call. She was distressed. An agency nurse, who worked at The Abbey, a private hospital as well as at the JR, had taken her aside. She accused Moss of being a danger to women. She says he does private work and Yasmin thought a lot were unnecessary surgical interventions. She wanted to report him but said the experience of whistle blowers in the NHS was not good. She asked if I knew a good journalist who might investigate him.'

'You wouldn't happen to know the name of the nurse?'

'No, she wouldn't give Yasmin her identity. Her comments made Yasmin look at some of his records. She believed that his reputation as a fast surgeon was justified but that the quality of that work had much to be desired. He implanted vaginal mesh for collapsed uteruses. Many women were left in long term pain. Yasmin believed he was being paid to promote the procedure by the manufacturers of the mesh.

'She wondered whether it would at least be worth discussing with him, the risks around the procedure. Do it tactfully quote some stats and ask his advice.'

'Do you know if she did?'

'I am so very sorry.' She started to cry.

'I've been a shit friend. I was too busy filming and enjoying myself over Christmas and New Year that I forgot to ring her and ask. I didn't even WhatsApp. I feel guilty. How could I be such a neglectful friend when she always went out of her way to help me?'

Mariam looked genuinely remorseful. Kate said,

'May I hold your hand?'

She nodded.

Kate put both her hands in hers and looked straight into her eyes.

'The last thing your friend will want is for you to feel guilty. The only guilty person is the person who killed her. Your information may help find whoever did it.'

Kate led Mariam back towards the dining hall saying,

'Nasreen and Jonathan will want to thank you for flying over from California. When do you have to return?'

'I only have two days in Oxford.'

'Here's my card. If there is anything else you remember, give me a ring.'

Ranjit sat by the lake thinking. He wasn't a religious man but his father was a serious turban-wearing Sikh and it looked like his son Roshan was taking after him. Ranjit thought about the compassion of the first Guru and vowed to appreciate his son's wishes and not do anything to deter him. He thought back to his time in the MET. It was soured by racism but there were colleagues he was grateful to. One detective he'd worked under for a short time, before he'd been moved to traffic, taught him a lot. CI David Jones told him to hang on to compassion.

'If you lose it, it's all too easy to become corrupted by the life you'll witness as a policeman. Be there for the good people. Care about them but, when a case has ended, shut it away in a mental drawer, otherwise you won't be able to do the job dispassionately.' He had pointed to his brain.

'You need that to be a fully functioning organ and not let the heart lead you astray.'

Ranjit thought about those words and also about Yasmin.

'How else do you function as a professional in these circumstances? But that can turn the victim into a *case*, not a living breathing personality.'

Ranjit wanted to hang on to the Yasmin Bell he now knew. He determined, from now on, not to forget the life that had been taken and that this delightful woman had been cruelly killed before she could fulfil her life.

Chapter 24

Like every morning, since the heavy machinery had appeared, George Gamble was observing the ongoing work in Radley Large Wood. He took photos to keep the campaigners informed.

His boots were becoming heavy with mud. Even the inveterate walker needed to tread with care to avoid falling and losing his boots in the quagmire. There'd been a period of dry weather so, by keeping to the side of the track, he was able to proceed. Ahead of him, a huge tree harvester was at work lifting piles of brushwood onto a lorry. George took out his phone to film it intending to post it on the Friends of Radley Large Wood Facebook page.

As he drew closer the workman was bending over to pick up a plastic package. The Coombes workers were used to seeing George around the woods and acknowledged him as he was about to dispose of it in a black sack in the front of the lorry.

'Looks like there's been some druggies hiding their gear,' he said, showing him the bag of medical waste. 'It was under that lot' pointing to the woodland waste.

'Wait mate, the police may be interested in that.'

'I don't want hassle.'

'Give it to me and I'll mark the spot where you found it. I'll tell them I found it.'

Once back home and divested of his muddy boots and trousers, George rang Kate.

***

Thomas Said had returned to London after Yasmin's Memorial Service. Ranjit rang him with the news.

'A local naturalist was walking behind Akaash's house this

morning and found a bag of medical waste. It contained bottles, scissors, a syringe, and a scalpel that could have been used on the victim.'

'It didn't look possible to walk there when we interviewed Akaash. Are you sure of the location?'

'Yes, it was under a giant woodpile about a hundred yards from the house. George Gamble is a friend of Kate's and a reliable witness. He was filming the workers in the wood loading the brash on to a lorry. When he hid it there, our murderer may not have been aware that kind of wood waste has value. It can be turned into electricity or wood chips.'

'Well done. This case may be solved sooner than you anticipated, Ranjit. Send it off to forensics. Would April Fool's Day be a good one to arrest Akaash Azad for abetting a murder?'

'I'm not sure we'll get results back by then.'

'You will if you mention us and explain that it's a matter of national security. They will make it a priority. That will give me time to complete a few investigations.'

'What time on April 1, can you come?'

'Arrest him early and let him sweat a bit? I'll be with you between 10.30 and 11. Make a bit of a joke of it, do you think?' suggested Thomas.

'What do I tell the team?'

'Down tools and enjoy the weekend and that includes you. You'll need someone on duty to be in touch with forensics and a uniformed guy to keep a look out on Akaash. Just don't go far and have the team stay on call.'

***

Jia could hardly believe it when Ranjit walked through the door at 5.30. The aromas coming from the kitchen were tempting.

'It's short notice but could we ask a few friends around tomorrow? I have the whole weekend off duty and so does Kate. I've never brought work home but I wondered whether it could be a good idea for you to get to know her. Her current best friend is the crime writer, Alex Hornby and, according to Kate, she's becoming friendly with the American scientist, Steve Darwin. He'll be speaking at the Oxford Literary Festival next week. I'll help cook and we could buy in the starters from Southall if we invite your ex-colleague, Amita to come and she could bring them? You said she liked Alex's novels. What do you think?'

'Why not? But check with Amber and Roshan first. I don't think they are expecting a taxi service but they sometimes don't tell me until the last minute.'

'Can we have a friend each too?' asked Amber, 'I'd like to meet Steve. After the mains we can escape to our rooms.'

It was agreed and Ranjit rang Kate and Alex. They'd been planning to see a film at the Ultimate Picture Palace but decided that seeing Ranjit on his home ground would be more interesting, so they accepted. Steve had intended seeing an old friend in London but persuaded him to come to Oxford on Thursday when he was speaking at the Sheldonian. So the party was on. Jia invited Amita and a new friend from Brookes.

'The numbers are growing. Luckily Indian food can stretch better than most European dishes. I'll start on the daal tonight – you can't cook that for too long...'

'The longer the better!' said the always calm and steady Jia.

***

The primroses and daffodils were out and the forsythia glowed like Moses' burning bush. Even the magnolia was in bud. The mature garden came with their Headington house and Ranjit was grateful. He wasn't brought up with a garden but enjoyed being outside in it. It was not high maintenance given the trees and shrubs. Ranjit found time to mow the circular lawn and Jia looked after the patio and pots. They only needed the gardener for a couple of hours a month to weed, feed and prune.

Guests arrived in warm early spring sunshine and were served drinks and starters in the garden. Their teenage children were happy to be waiters and enjoyed the praise they received.

'I've seen you before,' said Kate to Roshan. 'Weren't you helping in that caravan serving hot soup to the homeless in St Aldates in the winter?'

Roshan looked embarrassed but nodded.

'Well done, you. That's impressive. I admire you for that, Roshan,' smiled Kate tossing her hair out of the way.

'Do you know what you want to do?'

'I like history but I'm not sure it's the best subject for a career.'

'You need to talk to Alex. She LOVES history and storytelling.'

In the meantime, Amber was in conversation with Steve Darwin. He asked her the same question as Kate did Roshan and she replied,

'Medicine, but I'm not sure what branch. Any recommendations?'

'Neurology? I'll be talking about my latest book on the evolution of the brain at the Literary Festival. I can give you and your friend complimentary tickets if it interests you?'

Amber beamed. She loved being treated like an adult.

The ground floor of the house was open plan, as it suited Indian style entertaining, and its dominating feature was a long and sturdy refectory table. Out came the butter chicken, Rogan josh, a huge pot of daal, spinach chilli paneer, bhurta, rice, a pile of roti and pots of pickle and raita. Ranjit was liberal with the wine and beer. When they were all sated and their senses roused, Jia put on some Bhangra music and teased Ranjit into dancing with her.

'Teach your friends to dance. Practice for Strictly?'

Kate was seeing a new side to her boss and an insight into a family life that she had not known. Steve and Alex threw themselves into the dancing. The three of them took a taxi home and Steve got out with Alex at Woodland Road. It didn't look like he intended to go back to Abingdon Way that night.

While they were clearing up Jia said to Ranjit,

'Kate is good looking with her hair down but there's a tinge of sadness about her.'

'She moved to Oxford from the MET after her divorce, two years before me. I don't think she's met anyone she wants as a permanent fixture. Maybe that's it,' said Ranjit. 'How about being her match maker?'

Chapter 25

On April Fools' Day at 6am, the peace of Thames Reach was shattered. A black Maria, two police cars and a motor bike blocked Ash Crescent and broke into Akaash Azad's house. He was arrested, cuffed and read his rights. He asked to phone his solicitor and was told he could from the station. His solicitor arrived at 10.30 followed by Thomas Said at 11. Kate watched the interview through the one way glass.

Said showed him photos of various Iranian men. Akaash shook his head at each one. At the final one he looked shocked and nodded.

'His name is Ali Hussein and we have reason to believe that he has been employed by the Revolutionary Guard. When did you meet him?'

'In gaol but he wasn't a political prisoner and he said his name was Ali Salaam.'

'Were you expecting him on February 28 or did he just turn up?'

Asaash's solicitor told him that he didn't have to answer that question.

Said laid another photo of Ali on the table. He was approaching 13 Ash Crescent. From the angle it looked like it was taken from a car.

'What do the Revolutionary Guard expect of you, Akaash?'

'No comment.'

'Just to house their operatives from time to time? That must have seemed no bad deal if it got you out of that hell hole that is Evin.'

'No comment.'

Thomas looked at Ranjit. Ranjit waved to Kate. She entered

and handed him the bag of medical equipment.

Ranjit put the exhibit in front of Akaash.

'This was found behind your house. You didn't expect it would ever be found under six feet of brash, did you?'

Blood visibly drained from Akaash's face.

Kate thought he looked genuinely shocked.

'You won't be surprised that Forensics found Yasmin's DNA on the scalpel. It looks rather damning, don't you think?'

'But I didn't kill Yasmin. I couldn't kill anyone let alone a lovely young woman like her.'

'If that is true then help us nail the guy who did it,' said Said.

'Can I talk to my client in private?' asked the solicitor.

'That can be arranged. We'll even send in coffee. How do you take it?

Half an hour later, Akaash confessed that he had agreed to accommodate strangers from Iran. Ali had indeed arrived unannounced on February 27 and slept overnight but didn't return in the evening. He asked no questions.

'I didn't think that running an occasional B&B would be a problem,' said Akaash.

'You will be remanded in custody and questioned again tomorrow. If your story checks out you'll be bailed.'

***

'What do I tell Yasmin's parents and the press?'

'You can tell Yasmin's parents that we have a suspect. For the moment, tell the press you are following leads and hope to be able to tell them more before the end of the month.'

'We will need to take Akaash with us to London and question him there about other people who may have stayed with him,' said Thomas.

'Well done. It's been a pleasure to work with you. There is one thing you can still help with. We can't account for that umbilical cord. Can we leave that and Jim Azad to you?'

It felt like an anti-climax.

Chapter 26

At the team meeting, Ranjit had pinned the picture of Ali Hussein on the board.

'It is looking as if this could be our culprit. He's an Iranian criminal released from prison early to carry out a little job for the Revolutionary Guard sending a warning message to the regime's opponents and campaigners living abroad. There is one snag and that is the mutilation and use of the umbilical cord. The theory is that they wanted us to think she was killed by the opponents of abortion. Whatever the truth, we need to find the source of Exhibit 1.'

Kate raised her hand.

'Would an Iranian criminal have been able to carry out that precision surgery?

'Good question. Maybe they trained him or he had help, a doctor of Persian descent maybe?'

Peter Jordan joined in:

'The most obvious source would be Akaash's cousin, Jim but from what you said yesterday, Akaash didn't know what his overnight lodger planned. Jim has the ability.'

Before they could celebrate only needing to tie up loose ends, Ranjit was called to the phone.

'I think you should take this Sir,' said Veronica Chen.

It was Dorothy Mead,

'I've bad news. Whatever brought Ali Hussein to the UK, it wasn't to kill Yasmin Bell, at least to do it himself. We are looking into whether it was possible that he facilitated it. But I doubt it. He's a criminal, a hit man not an organiser. At the time of the murder, he was at Heathrow getting ready to board a plane to Tehran.'

'So we are back to square one? What about Akaash?

'We aren't going to charge him. He's agreed to cooperate with us in the future. He'll pass on pictures and info on his visitors. As a pharmaceutical agent who speaks Farsi and Arabic, he could be useful. You've met him, he's doesn't strike us as capable of that kind of murder and he has an alibi. He was at a conference at 3.30pm, so unlikely to have had time to kill her and get rid of the body without help.'

Ranjit didn't tell the team that Akaash had been recruited as a double agent but instead suggested they concentrate on their US visitors, Darcy Moss and Barbara Covet. Ranjit liked to play chess with Amber and Roshan. The game helped hone his strategic thinking. He hoped he wasn't facing defeat but it felt at best like stalemate.

Chapter 27

Armed with her complimentary ticket, Alex went to listen to her now close friend, Steve Darwin speak in the beautiful surroundings of Christopher Wren's Sheldonian Theatre. It was the last few days of the Oxford Literary Festival and although Alex regretted not being invited to speak herself, she'd attended several talks.

Once seated to one side of the auditorium, she looked opposite at the audience and saw Ranjit's daughter Amber enter with a friend. They seated themselves next to some female students who, judging from their scarves, were from Lady Margaret Hall. There were still twelve minutes before the start of the talk but Alex was not bored. Being an author, she was a people watcher.

She watched as a young man probably in his early twenties but, unusually for his generation, wearing a suit and tie, climb the steps and sit behind the girls. One of them, an attractive but tiny young woman of South Asian appearance, looked disturbed by his presence. She turned to her friends and together they got up and edged their way past Amber back on to the steps. The hall was filling up: the only remaining seats were in the gods. To get there, they had to leave the auditorium and use the outer stairs. Alex watched the young man go after them.

It took Alex a couple of minutes to cross to the other side and follow them to the upper gallery. She heard a disturbance and saw him towering over the girl, who looked up and said,

'I've told you over and over that I'm not interested. I'm not leading you on.'

Alex got between them,

'Is this guy harassing you?'

The student appeared grateful for Alex's intervention.

'Thank you. I met Gideon at a conference and chatted but

ever since he's been pursuing me. I keep telling him that I'm not interested in that kind of relationship but he won't take 'No' for an answer.'

'So that's Gideon Shriver,' thought Alex.

Alex told him to leave them alone and return to the lower tier of the theatre or she would report him for stalking. He looked angry but obeyed. When Alex returned to her seat, she was upset to see Gideon sitting behind Amber.

Steve's talk was well received and the organisers took him off for a meal. Alex noticed Gavin McGeorge and his London colleague join them.

Once outside, Alex rang Kate and told her what she had witnessed.

'Thank you. That is useful and the timing is perfect.'

***

Kate knocked on Ranjit's door.

'We have a lead, Sir.'

'That means we have two leads to follow. Remember the conversation with Yasmin's actress friend. I've got Chen looking into Darcy Moss and I've been doing some research around the issues she raised. Now we have something on Gideon Shriver whose mother is living with Moss. I didn't lie to the Chief Constable and the press, when I announced we are following leads even if the Iranian one has met a brick wall.'

***

Peter Jordan knocked on the door and joined them. He handed Ranjit a photo.

'That's Darcy Moss's car at Chandling's Manor at 4 pm on Feb 28!'

Chapter 28

Ranjit called a team meeting.

'Darcy Moss's car was parked close to where the body was found on the day of her murder and he is perfectly capable of using a scalpel with skill. He calls himself the fastest gynaecologist in England.'

Ranjit pointed to another picture.

'Gideon Shriver is of interest. He was caught harassing some female students at the Sheldonian. It has all the appearances of stalking and you will recall that Yasmin thought she was being followed.'

Pointing to Serena's pic, he said,

'I've been looking into their relationship. She and Moss met at a Pro-Natalist Conference in 2023. She has speaking engagements in most major cities aiming to promote the movement in the UK.'

'What is Pro-Natalism, Sir?' asked Chen.

'They regard the low birth rate in western countries as big a threat to humanity as climate change and some of their chief supporters prefer to undermine that threat to human life. In a nutshell they want women to have more children.'

Kate waved her hand.

'I suggested you take a look at Margaret Atwood's *Handmaids Tale,* Sir. In it ... '

'We're not at your book club, Sergeant. Let's stick to fact not fiction.'

Kate had wanted to talk about key Pro-Natalist supporters including Kevin Dolan, Simone and Malcolm Collins, and Elon Musk who, in their alt-right circles, talked about the "white-baby challenge". Some urged women to forget college and breed babies. To her that looked like the scenario of Margaret Atwood's fictional land of Gilead. Was it a coincidence that the female champion of Gilead in the novel was called *Serena?* Kate felt undermined for the first time in this case. She didn't want it to damage her relationship with Ranjit but, if he cared about his daughter, he ought to be concerned, but he was for moving quickly on.

'We must consider bring in Moss in for questioning. We know that Yasmin planned to speak to him but don't know if she did. We know that he's against abortion and his car was parked close to where the body was found. That is probably justification enough to bring him in but I'd prefer to visit him at his home. He's an influential man and I don't want to upset the Chief Constable unnecessarily. It keeps coming back to exhibit 1. He pointed to the photo of the umbilical cord. If we could link him with that, then we have a case.'

Kate raised her hand again.

'I'd like to look into Gideon. Can Richard dig into his social media? If he's an Incel and we have reason to believe that he is – then, there's a chance, that he could be involved.'

Ranjit agreed. Peter and Chen would look into Darcy Moss and Kate into Gideon. Richard would look for both of their mobile phones' locations.

***

Kate consulted Richard.

'Could you find out what kind of websites Gideon looks at?'

'Sure. That won't take long. Come back at four this afternoon.'

Kate saw Chen beavering away on her computer and waved to her. They'd worked closely together on the Price murder but this time felt different.

'Have I upset you, Veronica?'

'No, why do you think that?

'We shared ideas and reactions on the Price case. We work in a male dominated environment. Although we're fortunate here and the guys treat us as colleagues and not as coffee makers, our perspective is sometimes different.'

'Let's meet in Wolvercote after work. Go for a walk on Port Meadow and chat. Then have a drink at the Plough.'

'Good idea, I appreciate it. I can get away at five thirty today. How about you?'

***

Kate loved the way that walking side by side took away any stress about talking.

'I'm finding this case disturbing. In some ways I wish it had been a political assassination because the alternative seems worse to me.'

'How do you mean?' asked Chen.

'I asked Richard to look into the websites Gideon uses. Have you heard of the Manosphere?'

'Of course I have. Do you think that, because I'm of Chinese ancestry, I'm not in touch?'

'Oh, Chen. Do you really feel that discriminated against?'

'Not discriminated. How could I as Ranjit got my promotion? But I often feel ignored.'

'How can we change that?'

'Perhaps it's not even so specific. We are the third largest minority in the country but have you noticed how invisible we are? I thought you were ignoring me. But you're right. We should be supporting each other.'

'Let's start by sharing thoughts on this case.'

It was a warm April evening so they bought drinks and sat outside the Plough at an isolated table where they couldn't be overheard. Veronica started,

'I've found a case. Six months ago, the Abbey received a complaint from a Jane Whittaker. Moss ruptured her uterus when operating on her. I couldn't find any record of what happened to her complaint. Richard looked at their financial records around that time. They paid her £50,000. He thinks she probably signed a non- disclosure agreement. He also says they haven't employed Moss since then.'

'You know that Mariam, Yasmin's actress friend said Yasmin was going to talk to him about some procedures she regarded as problematic. It concerned the use of vaginal mesh for collapsed uteruses. Often patients are left in long term pain. I wondered if she also knew about the Whittaker case?'

'Obviously I'd like to interview Whittaker, but given the NDA, that may not be easy.'

'You could promise her that she will remain anonymous but at least get her to confirm the NDA. Run it by Ranjit.'

'You were saying about the Manosphere?'

'Gideon is all over it and not just the Andrew Tate show. It's become amplified since the Trump election. He and Musk believe they have the right to teach us family values! Men who've had seventeen kids with six different women! Gideon as well as following his Mum's pal, JD Vance, likes Nick Fuentes. Fuentes is more in his age group: he's only two years older than Gideon and has a huge following. He calls himself a Christian Nationalist and claims ownership of women's bodies.

'Your body, my choice' is his slogan. He supports the Nazi idea of Kinder, Kuche, Kirche. The site *Get back in the kitchen* is getting millions of views on X. At Texas State University, a man held up a sign that read *Women Are Property* and even middle school boys are chanting their slogans.'

'You're right to be concerned.' said Chen 'It's impacting here, too. Last week Kyle Clifford was found guilty of killing his girlfriend for rejecting him. He was active on Andrew Tate's War Room. He not only killed his girlfriend but her mother and sister too. They'd befriended him before they realised that he wasn't good for her,' said Veronica.

'Don't you think Gideon's different from most of the loners those sites target? He can't be lacking in confidence,' asked Kate.

'He could be more like Tate himself. Gideon is often in the eye of the camera. Tate grew his fame on Big Brother. They removed him from the show when he beat a woman with a belt. They justify violence as a means to control women. Richard says that he'll need a warrant to access Gideon's emails and his computer to see what he's been accessing on the dark web.'

'This feels daunting but important. We girls must stick together when the guys start to banter!'

Chapter 29

'We need to pay a visit to Mr Moss. Inspector Chen, ask when's a convenient time to call,' ordered Ranjit.

****

'Thank you for seeing us, Mr Moss.'

'You're welcome but I hope this can be brief.'

'Can we sit down and ask you a few questions?'

He showed them into the dining room.

'I was surprised that you weren't at the memorial to Dr Bell.'

'I sent her parents my apologies. I had hoped to attend but work got in the way.'

'Talking work, Mr Moss, I understand that, a week before her death, Yasmin Bell wanted to talk to you on some few work-related issues. Did that conversation happen?'

Moss shifted in his seat.

'We had a professional disagreement.'

'May I ask what it was about?

'She wanted the department to stop offering vaginal mesh treatments. Some patients suffered some unfortunate side effects but the procedure is life transforming for others. A balance of risks really.'

'I understand that you accidentally perforated a patient's uterus when carrying out an operation like that at the Abbey' said Chen.

Moss shifted uncomfortably in his chair.

'What has that to do with Yasmin Bell?'

'Maybe that was one of the side effects that concerned her?'

'I'm happy to help you look for Yasmin Bell's murderer but if this interview is going to continue in this vein, I'll call my lawyer before answering any more questions.'

'We've only two more questions and one I expect you can clear up.'

Ranjit handed him the photo of his car at Chandlings Manor.

'Is this your car? '

'Yes.'

'It was parked at Chandlings Manor School at 4.40 on the day Yasmin died and close to where her body was found.'

'That looks bad but it was a simple coincidence. You are aware that Serena Shriver is staying with me. She spends much of the week travelling the country giving talks but I offered to organise a weekend party of some local residents who would like to meet her. I dropped off an invitation to the head of Chandlings Manor. I knew the previous owners and they were on the guest list so I thought I'd ask her, too.'

'Did the party happen? Did she come?'

'Yes and yes. You can ask her to confirm it. If that is all...'

'One last question.'

'Gideon Shriver? What can you tell us about him?'

'He doesn't have his mother's charisma or persuasive ability but she is ambitious for him to have a political career. He appears to share her dream. She's of the opinion that a PhD from Oxford will add to his status. It would help if he could relate to people more easily. He seems to spend half his life on his phone. He told me you went to Richmond College to interview him so I'm sure you will have formed your own opinion.'

'Thank you, Sir. We'll leave you in peace.

***

The next morning at the team meeting, Chen was able to confirm that the head teacher received the invitation on February 28 and attended the party. Ranjit summed it up:

'Mr Moss had a motive to shut up Yasmin Bell and had the opportunity. We can place his car at Chandlings Manor where he could have dumped her body. It was conveniently parked out of sight of the school windows about forty yards from the lake.'

'A dead body is quite heavy, Sir, even someone as petite as Yasmin Bell,' said Kate.

'That's a problem. We didn't find any evidence of her body being dragged. But what is more of a problem, is how to find any evidence that would satisfy the Crown Prosecution Service.'

'There is no CCTV on the roads in Thames Reach so we have no evidence that he was there.'

'Richard can you track his mobile phone signals for that day?

'I expected you'd ask that, Sir.'

'In the morning, he was at the JR and in the afternoon his phone was at his house apart from the short drive to Chandling's Manor. He made a few other calls in the area with time slots that agree with delivering invitations.'

'Our only option is to inspect his car for forensic evidence.'

Chapter 30

When his car was towed away, the consultant vowed to complain to the Chief Constable.

On Friday morning, Ranjit reported to the Chief Constable. Ranjit wished Chief Constable Rayner had not taken early retirement. He suspected that the new Chief Constable would not have appointed him. He seemed more concerned about the possible publicity than about seeking the truth.

Kate asked Ranjit if they had the manpower to put a tail on Gideon.

'At least after six, Sir. Given his opinions, we need to take him seriously.'

'Six to ten pm starting next Tuesday. He'll be under his mother's thumb this weekend so you can organise the surveillance on Monday. I'm not sure what else we can do until we get the forensic report on Moss's Mercedes.

'I'll be in Jia's good books. A cousin's daughter is getting married this weekend. Her family have hired a hotel near Heathrow. It looks like I can go with her and the twins.'

'Have a good time sir.'

'It won't lend itself to quiet reflection. The disco they've hired is high volume. No choice but to dance. Most guests are staying overnight but I've told Jia that we must leave at 11 pm, so I won't drink. I'll need to be on call.'

'What about you? Any plans for the weekend?' asked Ranjit.

'It's the end of the Literary Festival and Alex has tickets for us. Given that my head is in a dysfunctional young man's mind, I've forgotten who we're going to hear. And we've booked a meal at that Caribbean restaurant near the Odeon. That'll be fun.'

***

Kate was pleased that she hadn't been called in and was able to walk with Alex and Steve on Sunday. Alex's son usually visited her one weekend a month but because he was working in Canada for three months, she was free. Kate realised that, unlike Alex, she was, according to Serena's hero, JD Vance, a 'cat lady'- childless and thus failing in her duty.

They glimpsed a family of rabbits on Thames Reach Meadow.

'What is it about the brain, Steve? I see a family of rabbits and it gets me thinking of Marcus. Mad, yes?'

'Associations. The rabbits look like happy families and you missed him last week – simple.'

For the first time in years, Alex had been alone on Mother's Day.

'Oh, I'm sorry Alex. Why didn't you say?' said Kate.

'Thanks, Kate, but Marcus called on WhatsApp and he's enjoying Montreal. He suggested I visit while he's there. Given what's happening in the States, I'm glad that he's in Canada especially as he isn't white. Oh, sorry Steve.'

'Talking Mother's Day. How's Sam? Mother's Day can be hard for a single mother,' asked Kate.

Steve replied,

'No need to worry: the Prices had a big get together at Kevin's house.'

'It's good to see the animosity towards her disappear. They saw how Godfrey had not left things easy for her and admire the way she's adapted. It was obvious to anyone that she adores her son and Goldie is adorable.' said Alex.

'What do you think of Vance and Musk's opinion that women like me are failing our duty?' asked Kate.

'There's not a shortage of human beings in this world. The

threat is to Nature, on which we depend to sustain life and we're destroying too much of it. If the population falls, life on earth will become more sustainable. So Kate - you are a heroine!' answered Steve.

'I guess the problem is around caring for an aging population and pensions. They are actually paid for by current-day workers and we have an imbalance,' said Alex.

'There are dangers associated with AI but that is where it could have a positive effect, if we had intelligent people in charge,' said Steve.

'Gee, we're putting the world to right. But the Yasmin Bell case shows how interconnected we are.'

'It's the Monarch butterfly effect,' said Steve.

They'd reached the cormorant tree but only one was perched at the very top, his wings hanging out to dry.

'I love the way his neck and beak point forward in that way, imperious but comic too,' said Alex. Steve looked at her appreciatively.

'Does that haughty entitlement remind you of anyone?' he laughed.

The image of Darcy Moss flashed in Kate's mind.

'Back to the brain and associations! Thank you, Steve,' said Alex.

On the fifteen minute walk back to Proof Social Bakery, they passed Sandford Lasher - a cut of the Thames. Alex looked at Steve.

'Remember when I told you that is probably the most dangerous stretch of water in Oxfordshire.'

She was thinking about how their eyes connected.

'Thames Reach is full of hidden gems.' He looked at Alex. 'And I'm glad I rented Sam's house. People told me I should stay in Summertown. This has been a pleasant rediscovery for me. It's changed a lot since I was a student.'

Kate was feeling the odd one out but worried what would happen when Steve's son and his family arrived in ten days' time.

Chapter 31

On Monday, Kate felt refreshed and invigorated and Ranjit looked how she felt.

'I could get used to having weekends off!'

She set about organising the surveillance of Gideon while Ranjit set up an interview with nurse Barbara Covet and asked the team to help him devise the questions.

In the afternoon, they received unwelcome news. Moss's car had come back clean with no evidence of having transported a body.

'It could mean that he didn't carry her or that she was so well wrapped in plastic, there were no traces left or that he knew how to clean it, to get rid of any tell-tale signs. Even if we find our murderer, pinning down evidence will be a killer.'

***

You could say their luck changed that evening but not for Sushila, the LMH student. Kate had asked Constable Jones to wear civilian clothes to tail Gideon. He watched as he jumped in front of her as she passed University Parks on her way back to college. Gideon pushed her through the gate and against the fence and tried to kiss her. She pushed him away.

'You unappreciative bitch! Don't you know who I am? Do you think I'm one of the 80 percent?'

Sushila had no idea what he was talking about. She took a deep breath and said:

'Attraction is not about influence. It's chemistry. I'm working hard for my degree and don't want a relationship. Leave me alone. Stop following me. I don't want to see again.'

She tried to get past him and onto Norham Road but he

grabbed her hard from behind and squeezed her breasts until she screamed with pain.

'That'll teach you,' he said in a soft but chilling tone.

The constable arrested him and told him his rights as he cuffed him. He got on the phone and summoned help.

In the station, Kate asked Sushila if she would give a statement and she agreed.

'I don't know what I would have done if your officer had not come to help me. There's no way of getting through to him. A two-minute friendly conversation over lunch at a conference and since then, he's acted as if owns me.'

Gideon knew HIS rights without them being read to him. His mother and an expensive lawyer arrived before they could interview him. In the meantime, they had confiscated his phone and Richard was busy looking at it.

'Look at this,' he said to Kate. 'He's on Dynamite with the pseudonym Childless Cat Lady Killer.

'Well done, Richard.'

The interview yielded nothing because the lawyer instructed Gideon to say 'No comment' to every question. His mother contacted the US Embassy and the Vice President.

***

Word was out of Gideon's arrest and his supporters were soon condemning the UK as godless with lack of respect for freedom of speech and harassing students of religion.

The Chief Constable hurried over and suggested they release Gideon on a caution to avoid an international incident. They returned his belongings, including his phone, and Ranjit said they would apply for a restraining order for him to stay away from Sushila and LMH.

He turned to Serena.

'I suggest you teach your son to respect women.'

Kate wondered if she should tell Ranjit that Gideon had sat behind Amber at Steve's talk but decided he had enough on his plate and not to add to his worries. She thought it unlikely that Gideon would know what school Amber attended.

Chapter 32

Alex rang Kate to plan their weekly pub night.

'Shall we go to Jericho? Steve and I'll take a walk along the canal to the Bookbinder's and meet you there?'

During the meal she whispered to them about her experience that day and of the frustrating unfairness of it all.

'It reminds me of the Bullingdon Club. Boris Johnson used to belong to it while a student here. They're mostly Hooray Henrys. Peter Jordan described how he was called out to a country pub where they'd climbed on tables, thrown furniture around and broken windows. Nothing came of the arrests because the landlord dropped charges when their parents compensated him generously. If working class kids did that, they'd have criminal records. It looks like Gideon will get away with his assault on Sushila. But we learned something useful from his phone: his pseudonym on *dynamite* is Childless Lady Cat Killer.'

Steve looked thoughtful.

'If you can't infiltrate his posts on it, without a warrant, there are people who can. They call themselves *ethical hackers.* The problem is, that unless you can access the same evidence legally, you wouldn't be able to use what you find.'

'Thank you Steve, I need to know. So, please, put me in touch with one. It could lead to trouble with Professional Standards but this underground Manosphere is leading to so much violence against women that I'm willing to risk it.'

***

'Please sit down Nurse Covet.'

'I don't understand why you want to see me again. My mother said you called and checked my alibi for 28 February.'

'That's correct and we know that you weren't in Oxford on the day of the murder, but we want to ask you about the complaint Dr Bell made against you.'

'It's simple really. She and I had different values. She was a champion of wokeness and I uphold family values.'

'Some say that *woke* is just another word for *empathy* and she claimed that you came across as judgemental when delivering the baby of an unmarried mother without a partner. Is that correct?'

'I'm a good midwife. I put safely first and we get overwhelmingly busy so I don't chatter as much as some.'

'Bedside manner is a matter of personal interpretation so let's leave it at that,' said Ranjit.

'Her other complaint concerned the removal of that patient's placenta and umbilical cord.'

Barbara looked rattled.

'You can talk freely: we're not here to pursue any charges related to it. You probably had good reason? And we would like to know your reasons - that's all.'

'Mr Moss asked me. He has friends doing research related to nutrition within the womb and wanted to compare mothers in different social situations. Since the placenta and cord are treated as hospital waste, I didn't see any problem.'

'Did you ask permission to take it out of the hospital?

'No, because I didn't take it out of the hospital – I put it in a sterile bag and then in a cool box and left it in Mr Moss's office. I had done it before for him.'

'Thank you, Nurse Covet, for clearing that up for us. You can go.'

***

'The evidence against Moss is mounting. We need DNA from that cord to see if it matches the birth mother.'

'In the meantime, let's go door to door in Woodland Road with pics of Gideon and Moss and of Moss's and Serena's cars to see if any one remembers seeing them.'

***

Constable Jones and Kate went door to door at the far end of Woodland Road. Most people in the houses near to Yasmin's home had been out at work on the afternoon of 28 February so it looked as if their return trip was not going to be fruitful. When Kate was coming out of No 131, George Gamble was walking in their direction.

'Am I allowed to ask what are you doing here?'

She showed him the photos of Moss and Shriver.

'It's not secret –the more residents who see these images, the better. We want to know if anyone saw either of them in Thames Reach on Feb 28 or around that time.'

George took a closer look at the picture of Shriver.

'That guy almost knocked me off my bike.'

'He was driving?'

'Yes, a big black Tesla. I thought he looked too young to own an expensive car like that. His clothes were unusual for his age too – another reason why I remember him. He parked at the circle at the end of the road and I cycled up to him as he was getting out. I told him - *Driving a car is a responsibility*, it can be a dangerous weapon. There's no damage done to me, but you've scratched my bike. If you'd passed that close to a child on a bike you could have injured her or worse she could have fallen under your wheels.' He offered me cash to paint my bike but I said I'll leave the scars on display.'

'George, you're a star. Thank you!'

'I should've told you before. He parked a hundred yards from her house so I didn't connect it to Yasmin.'

'Did you notice if he was carrying anything.'

'Yes I did. Unusual for a guy his age: it was a briefcase.'

Kate rang Ranjit and explained that George was an observant birdwatcher and his identification could be relied upon. A few clicks and it was confirmed that Serena Shriver drove a black Tesla.

***

'I want both of them brought to the station. Let's give it one more day to prepare the interviews and find more links to connect them to the crime. I must forewarn the Chief Super but keep it as low key as possible. Don't tell the press. Unmarked cars and no uniformed officers to bring them in.'

Unfortunately no one told that to Serena Shriver.

Chapter 33

Moss and Shriver were in separate interview rooms. Ranjit and Chen were going to lead on Moss with Kate and Peter on Shriver. The interviews were to take place at different times so they could also observe the reactions.

First up was Moss. His solicitor arrived minutes after he'd been checked in. As he was led away, he'd asked Serena to contact him. The questioning had not even begun when Constable Jones knocked on the door. Ranjit left the room.

'Sorry to disturb you sir but a crowd's gathering outside and the Chief Constable is on the phone.'

He looked out of a window to see that Serena Shriver had rallied a group of her supporters and was addressing them through a loudspeaker. The local press and freelance photographers were busy taking photographs and at least one journalist was recording on his phone to *live* feed. It was just a matter of time before the paparazzi would join them.

Ranjit took the call.

'Serena Shriver has been staying with Moss in Boars Hill so was quick off the mark. It's only be matter time before national press and photographers arrive. I'm sorry, Sir, but you could have public order issues to deal with,' said Ranjit, trying to sound in control.

'Make your interviews as short as possible and get them out through the back door. I'm on my way to Kidlington now and will want a statement to read to the crowd and to ask them to leave but they are unlikely to take any notice.'

'Keep it simple, Sir. Shriver and Moss are helping with our inquiries into the murder of Dr Yasmin Bell.'

'I hope for your sake, Singh that these interviews are worth it.'

***

Geoff Hunter, reporter from the Daily Post was on the next train to Oxford Parkway only a short walk from the Thames Valley Police HQ. A row of policemen and women wearing high viz, kept the crowd at a distance from the gates but they were spilling over onto Oxford Road. The police were struggling to contain them so they brought in orange fencing and stationed officers to keep the traffic moving. Serena had taken a break and was on the phone to the US Embassy. Given the time lapse, the US was waking up to the news that her son had been arrested. Hunter sent his card to her through her supporters asking for an interview and she agreed. They arranged to meet over coffee in the nearby shopping precinct in twenty minutes.

Hunter couldn't believe his luck, this felt like a scoop.

***

'Thank you, I need that.'

Serena looked exhausted as she took the coffee from him and the pain au chocolat looked welcome too.

'It's been a long morning.'

'What did they charge them with?'

'They charged Moss with the murder of this woman. I disagreed fundamentally with her opinions but I didn't for one minute wish her dead. A distinguished surgeon accused of her murder. What has happened to the justice system in this country?'

'And your son?'

'Abetting a crime.'

'Have they any evidence of that?'

'Of course not. All I know is that it relates to my TESLA because they have taken it to examine. He borrowed it on the day she died. That is pretty flimsy to me.' Her phone rang.

'I must take this, it's the Vice President.'

***

Hunter got on the phone to his editor. In no time at all, the Mailon-line'headlined his story.

The US Vice President, the anti-abortion campaigner and a death in Oxfordshire.

Hunter reminded them that the victim lived in the village where two suspicious deaths had taken place two years ago. As he finished his report, a red light lit up in his head. The world's press would gather here at the Thames Valley Police HQ, none of them would go to Thames Reach where the victim lived.

'When that developer was murdered, I picked up a great line from that crime writer woman...'

He called a taxi and headed for Alex Hornby's house.

***

Alex was surprised to see him. Their interview had turned out well last time, so she let him in. It couldn't do her book sales any harm. He started diplomatically by asking about her writing.

'I'll be able to tell you more on Friday. An exclusive? Cheetah will hopefully confirm that they're going to televise my books. You could be having coffee with the next Ann Cleeves. I shouldn't have said that. Please don't quote me. I'm a huge admirer of her writing. If I'm a patch on her skill, I'll be pleased.'

'Publicity for you and your books can't hurt though, can it?'

'You're right. There was a boost in my sales after your article during the Price investigation.'

'You guessed right. Another murder has brought me here.'

'Dr Bell, I presume?'

'Did you know her? I believe she lived on this road.'

'I only met her once but Sam Price knew her because she was a client at her gym.'

Alex described how Sam had to struggle financially and set up her business. Alex assumed that some publicity wouldn't be bad for her, either.

'May I have the number of Yasmin's house so I can take a photo of it?'

Alex was starting to feel anxious. She shouldn't trust this man but, as he could find the address in other ways, she told him.

Hunter walked down the road and took a selfie in front of Yasmin's house in Woodland Road and sent it to the paper with him recording a message.

'This was the home of Dr Yasmin Bell in a quiet road in the quiet village of Thames Reach but was it also where she was murdered? Her body was found by local toad patrollers in a nearby pond. Guess who found it? That murder victim hunter, the crime writer Alex Hornby, who just happens to live on this road.'

A colleague on Daily Post rang him.

'No, *she* didn't tell me but it came from a reliable source.'

As he rang off, Geoff said to himself,

'Thank you Constable Jones. You earned your fee.'

Then he started to live stream.

'This morning, all hell broke loose outside of the Thames Valley Police Headquarters when two prominent citizens were taken in for questioning relating to the murder of Dr Yasmin Bell. One of them was a distinguished consultant but what has caused the crowds is the identity of the other man. Gideon Shriver is the son of Serena Shriver the anti-abortion activist and campaigner for JD Vance, the Vice President of the USA. I can confirm that she spoke to him on the phone this morning. Are we witnessing a diplomatic incident in the making? This is Geoff Hunter, reporting from Thames Reach in Oxfordshire.'

He walked through to the alley that joined Woodland Road to

Abingdon Way and headed towards the Price fortress. When he arrived, he hardly recognised it. Sam had transformed it. He took a photo before ringing the bell.

'Can I help you?'

'My name is Geoff Hunter.' He held out his hand to shake hers.

'I've just come from your friend Alex Hornby. She says you may be able to help me. She said Yasmin Bell was a client of yours.'

Sam invited him in.

'What can you tell me about Dr Bell?

'Not much really. She was a very busy woman. Her post was joint NHS and Oxford University but you probably know that. To keep up the pace, she needed to be fit. She loved nature and running in Radley Large Wood which was why she joined the campaign to stop the further felling of ancient trees. She joined the gym because what we offer helped her relax as well as keep fit.'

At that moment, Steve Darwin got out of the swimming pool and walked through the conservatory. Hunter recognised him from somewhere.

'Oh, Steve, this is Geoff Hunter. He's a journalist. Alex sent him. He's writing a piece on Yasmin.'

Steve looked suspicious.

'What paper do you write for?'

'The Daily Post'

'Look, Sam. Take some advice from me. Terminate this interview.'

As he left, Geoff turned and took a quick picture of Steve. Outside, he searched for likenesses and knew he was onto another good story.

Chapter 34

'What a coincidence that one of Serena Shriver's and the Republican National Coalition for Life's (RNCL) most effective opponents is currently living in Thames Reach. This story is becoming stranger than fiction.'

Hunter's report in the Mailonline was shared and shared and spread worldwide.

***

Alex was horrified. She had been working on her computer when a news flash caught her eye. She was looking at a photo of Steve at No 1 Abingdon Way. Beside it was a link to a video of Serena Shriver at a Campaign to Save America railing against Professor Darwin as the symbol of everything that was wrong with the country. She was laying the blame on him for turning the nation's concerns and her heroes into jokes.

She watched another YouTube video in which Steve was lampooning Serena crowning King Donald with joker JD watching on. Steve was holding a Banksy-like cartoon which mirrored the David portrait of Napoleon taking the crown from the Pope's hands to crown himself. No-one was to be seen as superior to Bonapart or Trump.

'Serena Shriver is delusional if she thinks she has influence over our would-be emperor. He will use her and discard her like he does everyone.'

Alex was riveted and clicked on more videos of Steve. In one, he held up a replica encyclopaedia. She enlarged the title: *The Encyclopaedia of Ignorance*, by Donald Dunce. There was Steve mouthing silly quotes, mimicking 'The Donald' in a faux-solemn manner as if from a real encyclopaedia, with his audience in stitches.

Alex guessed that Serena knew that ironic humour undermined the president and her. But for Alex it was like a light had come on: it dawned on her that she was falling in love with Steve. Her mood changed dramatically when she remembered Geoff's report.

'How did he know that I found the body – I didn't tell him?'

She was straight on the phone to Sam.

'How could you send that man here, Alex? My house is surrounded by press and photographers from all over the world. It's putting my clients off. They don't want to fight their way through the pack and Steve is leaving. He says they'll go away if he goes away.'

'I am so sorry Sam. I didn't direct him to you but I did say that I met Yasmin at your gym.'

Sam sounded tearful but forgiving.

'I can't talk now Alex. When things calm down, let's meet.'

Alex rang Steve on his mobile to apologise.

'Why did you talk to that man?'

Alex tried to explain but it made no difference.

'My ex will not let my grandsons come here to be at the centre of harassing media attention. I have no choice but to leave.'

'Oh, Steve! Where will you go?'

'I'm going to Paris on Eurostar this evening and they'll fly there at the weekend. It was nice knowing you, Alex. I wish you all good things. We can stay in touch by email.'

Alex was in tears, a sharp contrast to Geoff Hunter, who was basking in the approval of his editor in chief.

Chapter 35

Under pressure was an understatement: Ranjit's instructions were to charge them or release Shriver and Moss asap. If this was a disaster, he knew he'd be the Thames Valley Police and government's sacrificial lamb offered for slaughter by the media. Ranjit wondered how that vision had come into his mind. He was, after all a Sikh, and that was a Christian image. Maybe the Easter eggs prominent in the supermarkets had reminded him. He felt mild relief from the numbing terror, as he entered the silent windowless interview room which kept the outside world at bay.

He started by going over old ground about Moss and Bell's professional interactions. Moss's solicitor interrupted to complain that,

'My client has already told you what he knows on this subject. This line of questioning is starting to feel like harassment.'

'We want to give Mr Moss the opportunity to tell us more on his own accord. Yasmin Bell's phone and laptop were the only things taken from her house. But Jim Azad has provided us with some of her emails. We know that Yasmin was about to report Mr Moss for unprofessional conduct.'

Moss nodded to his solicitor.

'Azad would say that wouldn't he?'

'Why?'

'He was the one she was accusing of unprofessional conduct. She suspected him of cooking up data.'

Ranjit decided to take a break and he allowed Moss and solicitor to have coffee. This was not going well.

'We have no reason to bring Jim Azad in, but Peter, set up a time when you can interview him where ever he likes. Get Richard on to him. Last time, he found nothing suspicious. Worth another go? Sam Price said Yasmin was upset before Christmas after meeting him, but Jim Azad said it was due to Moss.'

Chen suggested they move on to the cord evidence.

'There's another reason we have brought you in. I've permission to give you some information that we haven't disclosed to the public and want to keep it that way. We want you and your solicitor to sign an agreement that you will not tell anyone else without our permission. It will be crucial in any trial.'

'This is most irregular.'

'It is but, when I give you the information, you will understand. It's the strongest evidence we have. If as you say, you are innocent, then you will be able to answer our questions.'

The solicitor asked to leave the room and talk to Chen. He signed a paper returned and advised his client to agree.

'What we have not told the parents or the press is that to all appearances Yasmin Bell had been strangled with an umbilical cord. That rather narrows down suspects.

'We interviewed Nurse Covet and she told us that you had asked her to provide the placenta and cord from a particular patient for research purposes. Is that correct?'

'No it isn't correct. Why would she say that?'

'She said that she left it in a cool box in your office. What have you to say about that?'

'Well, I didn't remove it from there. I suggest you ask Azad?'

Ranjit was all too aware of the Chief Constable's insistence on short interviews and he wasn't sure that any more could be achieved.

'We'll agree to follow up your comments and let you leave. However, there's a condition that you stay in the country and that your solicitor keeps in touch about your movements.

'I suggest you leave from the back in an unmarked police car, if you don't want to be mobbed by photographers.'

***

'Was Jim Azad hiding something or was Moss planting a red herring?'

Ranjit asked his team their opinion when his phone rang. Ranjit let the Chief Constable know that Moss had left the building and they were about to interview Gideon.

'This has exploded. It's become international news. The responsibility for any repercussions will be firmly on your shoulders, DCI Singh.'

Chapter 36

Moss's solicitor was highly regarded in the local scene, but Gideon's representative was in another league altogether. Kate opened the interview.

'Mr Shriver, we hope that we don't need to keep you long. You can help us by answering a few questions.'

'For your sake, I hope you have good reasons for dragging my client here under duress. This is not good for relations between this country and the government of the USA.'

Kate handed him a photo taken on the ring road of Gideon driving his mother's car near the turning for Thames Reach.

'Is this you?'

He nodded.

'This was taken less than an hour before we believe Yasmin Bell was murdered and we have a witness who says you knocked him off his bike while driving on Woodland Road. Would you like to tell us about that? Why were you outside Dr Bell's house?'

His solicitor shook his head.

'No comment.'

'She took out the picture of him yelling at Yasmin Bell at the anti-abortion demonstration at the JR.'

'This is you?'

He nodded.

'You made it clear what you think of her, so why visit her?'

His solicitor shook his head.

'No comment.'

The interview proceeded in the same way for fifteen minutes prompting Kate to take a break. She went to get some coffee and looked at her phone there had been a missed call from Steve Darwin. Why was he ringing? She decided to call him back.

'I'm sorry that I have to leave Oxford. Alex was indiscreet with a red top journalist so 1 Abingdon Way is besieged with journalists wanting to talk to me. I'm leaving because I can't have my grandsons exposed to this. But before I go, I'll send over the file from my ethical hacker. I'm not going to reveal his identity but you'll appreciate what he's found. You can show these images to Gideon but not use them in court unless you get a warrant to access them yourself. I hope you nail the villain.'

***

Kate could hardly believe what she was seeing and gestured to Ranjit. This was the breakthrough they needed.

'Where did you get this?'

Kate explained.

'I was aware that I can get in trouble. It is unorthodox but my hunch was right, Sir.'

'The problem is his solicitor. He'll want to know and then you'll be subject to a professional standards inquiry. We need to think quickly. Let's get Richard onto this. It could take time and I don't think we have that. We can't confront Gideon and his solicitor with it until we've sourced it legitimately. Given the political pressure, we can't keep him here much longer. But I have an idea.'

Ranjit approached the solicitor.

'You know about the nuisance occurring outside. I don't want your client to have to cope with the press en masse. If we say you have left the premises, they will get bored and leave and the government will be relieved. Can we agree to postpone the interview and continue it somewhere else tomorrow?' He agreed.

Later that day, the team re-watched the video. Gideon was boasting that he had taken *the red pill* and here was the proof that he could lead them and become the Authentic Voice of Man. Wearing blue surgical gloves, he was waving the umbilical cord like a lasso over what looked like Yasmin's body. Her face was not showing so that could be a problem. But in the corner, was someone else's hand.

'You do know whose hand that is? There are not many men with such perfectly manicured nails and not many unmarried men who wear rings. I believe that fish symbol has religious significance.'

'It could be his but I trust your observations more than my own when it comes to visual detail. My idea is not exactly ethical, either. If it doesn't work we'll both be suspended. Let's ask Richard to manipulate the image so some of Yasmin's head is showing and then we will confront Moss with it.' His phone rang. It was Dorothy Mead.

'You have opened a can of worms, DCI Singh. There's no way of putting the wiggly things back inside and sealing it. Getting extradition from Iran is impossible but extradition from the USA is not easy, either. I'm ringing to warn you that your suspect maybe about to bolt.' She hung up.

Ranjit asked the chief constable to inform immigration to stop Gideon leaving the country.

Chapter 37

The next day, the black Tesla was returned but, when Ranjit and Kate arrived in Boars Hill, it was not in the drive. Darcy Moss spoke abruptly,

'They left at ten this morning. I have given you enough of my time. If you want to ask me more questions, I'll call my solicitor.'

'Please do. But first can we come in and show you some video? You may want to tell him about it, when you ring him.'

Showing some reluctance, Moss ushered them in.

'I'm sorry to say that your guest's son is active on the dark Incel web and posted this video to like-minded *dynamite*, as they label themselves. He thought we couldn't find it. Childless Cat Lady Killer is his tag. But you will see that there were two people present in this clip and we believe that hand is yours Mr Moss. Our tech people will extract enough of your finger whorls for forensics to identify you.'

After watching the film, Moss's demeanour changed. Ranjit and Kate could hardly believe what they were witnessing. This cold composed man was crying.

'I can't face my God with this weighing on my conscience.'

Ranjit waited patiently then said,

'There is something you would like to confess?'

Moss looked like a humbled man not used to doubting his judgement.

'Serena was worried about Gideon and asked me to be a father to him while he's in Oxford. I don't have children of my own and I took it seriously. I told him to ring me at any time he needed help and that my door would always be open to him, even if he was in trouble. It's not a justification for what I did but it is an explanation. I deserve anything that is coming. Just know that is why it happened.'

'Thank you for being honest with us. We appreciate that this will not be easy for you but can you tell us what happened on February 28 and give us permission to record it? I must read you your rights and this would be a good time to call your solicitor,' said Ranjit.

'I'd prefer to tell you now and, yes, you can use it as evidence. Let's go in the dining room and sit at the table where you can record me.'

***

As a Sikh, the confessional was a mystery to Ranjit but he had a strong feeling that Moss was using him like a priest; that he hoped confessing would bring absolution.

'Gideon called me from Yasmin Bell's house and asked if I could come because there'd been a terrible accident. When I arrived, he let me into the lounge. Yasmin was dead on the floor. He sounded sorry for himself saying,

"I didn't mean to kill her. I wanted to teach her a lesson."

I asked him how he came to be there. I made him sit down because he was pacing around the room and was about to bang his head on a wall. I said: "I promised that I will be like a father to you, so tell me everything and I'll do my best to help you."

'This is what Gideon told me:

"I got her phone number from Barbara Covet and rang her on a burner phone. I pretended to be a delivery driver and wore that mask and wig so she wouldn't recognise me. I had this device to distort my voice. As soon as she opened the door, I jabbed her with a needle and drugged her. It worked quickly. She staggered and I pushed her on the floor.'

He stopped talking so I put my hand on his and said,

"Are you trying to tell me that you raped her?"

He started to sound sorry for himself.

"I hadn't meant to.' He took a plastic tube containing a scalpel out of his pocket.

"This was to cut her clit. I wanted to preserve it to remind me that this woman could never enjoy sex with anyone ever again. But seeing her lying there helpless, I couldn't stop myself. I ...I'm 23 but until thirty minutes ago was a virgin. Afterwards, it felt good to lay satisfied on top of her. She didn't move so I didn't realise that I'd smothered her or it could have been the drugs. I tried to pump her chest, tried to bring her back. What can I do? They'll know I did it. They'll have my DNA."

'I'd made a solemn promise to his mother, but why did I help him and not ring you? I've been asking myself that ever since.'

Moss took a deep breath and continued.

'In that moment, Gideon looked ashamed of what he'd done. I told him to help me get her into the bath. I operated on her to remove evidence of the rape. I flushed the medical waste in tiny pieces down the toilet and then filled it with bleach. There was a plastic shower curtain in a cupboard in the bathroom. I told him to help me wrap her in it. I explained what we needed to do with the body.

"Evidence will be removed in water but there will be too many people walking and running by the Thames but no-one at Chandlings pond."

'Her house is a semi-detached so I was able to bring the car up her drive close to the back door. It wasn't difficult getting the body into the boot without being seen. We cleaned everything thoroughly but I impressed on him that he had to come back wearing PPE and clean everywhere with surgical detergents. The lounge was hardwood. I told him to bring a hand held vacuum and make sure there was not a single hair to be found anywhere. I took the key out of the door and gave it to him.

'In the garden shed I found some thick black plastic sheeting of the type used under pebble drives. A bit left over, I presumed. I put that in the boot and we laid the body on it. I wrapped her in that too. The party invitations were in the car. That was all true.

'I told him to get on the floor behind the passenger seat and make sure he wasn't seen. It had to look as if I was alone when we drove into Chandlings Manor at dusk. They have CCTV. I delivered the invitation and returned to the car knowing that we could carry the body to the pond under the cover of darkness. Close to the bridge we'd be unlikely to be seen from the school. That's what happened. So now you know the truth.'

'You've missed out something surely–the umbilical cord,' said Kate.

'Yes, that. I had just put the cool box in the car when he rang me. It was indeed intended for research. Seeing it there, it occurred that it could disguise the smothering and maybe lead you on a wild goose chase. I told him to strangle her with it. I was leaning over her pushing the lower part of her body into the water and didn't see the fool take that selfie.

'He tied it around her neck tightly and we left and, yes, I took the car for a valet clean the next day and followed that up with disinfectant. But her body was so well wrapped that I was confident that it would reveal nothing.'

'I presume you took her phone and laptop,' said Ranjit.

'They are somewhere in landfill. I put them in black sacks containing general household waste ready for collection on the Thursday morning. I'd removed the SIM from the phone and smashed the computer.'

'We'll charge you with the mutilation of a body and obstructing justice. As you have confessed and will plead guilty, you can expect a more lenient sentence.'

'We will allow you time to call your housekeeper and solicitor and the hospital. Then we must take you to the station. We'll type up your statement and get you to sign it. Tomorrow morning, we'll take you to the Magistrates Court where you can apply for bail. We won't oppose conditional bail.'

Ranjit sent out the order to arrest Gideon and to charge him with the rape and murder of Yasmin Bell. As they drove past Jonathan and Nasreen Bell's house, Ranjit remembered that her parents were unaware of the mutilations to Yasmin's body. The pathologists had carefully sewn her up and put her in a leotard before dressing her and sending her body to the funeral directors. He would have to tell them everything. He had been finding excuses not to.

'How do you tell a parent that such horrors were committed on their daughter?' he asked Peter, knowing that he too had children.

Chapter 38

Peter Jordan walked in.

'I did as you asked, Sir: interviewed Jim Azad.'

Strange how irrelevant that feels when only a few days ago... thought Ranjit.

'What did he say? Did you get an explanation?'

'Yep. Your instinct was right. He and Akaash are closer than either of them admitted. He was adamant that he knew Akaash's character and that, no way, would he have killed Yasmin. But, he suspected what we now know to be true that, to get released from Evin prison, he'd made an agreement. That's why he'd been so guarded. He was trying to protect his cousin.'

'This case... the network of relationships. Thanks Peter. Good job. I've a call to make to the powers that be.'

Ranjit contacted Dorothy Mead to tell her about Moss's confession. On the basis of his account of events on February 28, they had tried to arrest Gideon but had been unable to find him or his mother. They still hadn't got a warrant so they couldn't use the video sent to them as evidence. Therefore, Ranjit relied on Moss's account of events. He described to Dorothy the evidence they were building of Gideon's activities on the dark web on sites which glorify violence against women.

'Would that be something that could interest you and you could help with?'

'That could be a waste of time. He left on a US Government plane out of RAF Fairford, two hours ago.'

'He *what*?'

'It's not unusual for US military planes to use Fairford.'

'Are you saying the US government helped him escape justice?'

'No comment on that one, but his mother has friends.'

'What can we do?'

'The Crown Prosecution Service will need to issue an extradition warrant but I warn you, it won't happen easily. We send the accused to USA without much hesitation but it will be almost as hard as if Iranians had done it to bring Gideon Shriver to trial in the UK. The Bells will have to be satisfied with convicting Moss. It looks like his faith trumped his self-interest. You owe Moss a lot DCI Singh. He's restored your reputation. I have a meeting so must go.' Mead terminated the call as undiplomatically as she had introduced herself two weeks earlier.

Ranjit was fuming. His eyes blazing, he shouted at Kate,

'They knew, they knew he was leaving and even knew where he was flying from and did nothing to stop him.'

She swore but then bit her tongue because Ranjit didn't swear. He called the team together.

***

'Its politics isn't it, sir? It's no wonder some in the force fall from grace,' said Peter.

'Talking about *falling from grace!* Someone in this building took a backhander from a reporter, to tell the world who found Yasmin's body,' said Kate.

'If anyone knows who that is please, don't protect him or her,' said Ranjit.

The team looked downhearted, so Ranjit tried to change the mood.

'Cheer up everyone. This case was daunting, with obstacles at every turn, and despite the mounting pressure we stuck to the search for the truth. The intelligence services didn't think there was an iota of a chance that we'd succeed. I wish I could guarantee that justice will be seen to be done or even that something good could come out of it, like curbing the way social media is twisting the hearts of isolated young men.'

'Is there anything we can do?' asked Veronica Chen.

'If the government won't do anything, is there any initiative possible in Oxfordshire?'

'Well said, Veronica. It's simpler than most people think. Boys need purpose and boys need love and friendship. Trends in society often mean they get neither of these. We see it all the time. The state is a lousy parent. A quarter of boys in care end up in trouble with us. It's all about safety checks and ticking boxes and not about providing purpose in their lives.'

He looked thoughtful.

'How about this? Let's liaise with schools and the remnants of the youth service and probation service and organise sports events. What do you think of this idea? We set up a station football team and challenge them to play us. Instead of lecturing them, we may get a chance to listen to them and mentor them.'

'I like the idea, Sir and I'd love to take part but will we be given the time and money to do it? I see little enough of my wife and children...' asked Peter.

'The Chief Constable should be pleased, so now's the time to ask. And we need to celebrate our achievement even if no one else does. Peter can you find out when and where everyone would like to go? Drinks on me.'

***

At Beechlands, Ranjit was shown into a sunny lounge. The owners looked like a shadow of their former selves, as if someone had switched off a light.

'Do you want to know everything?'

'We'd appreciate the truth' said Jonathan.

'Then this will take a while,' and he began.

Jonathan wasn't surprised or even angry that Gideon had got away. Jonathan Bell had been a diplomat and seen it all before. But Nasreen was bitter.

'I escaped one misogynistic regime and was optimistic that their days were numbered. I didn't see the likes of Vance coming. I fought back against the Mullahs but Trump's Gilead has destroyed me. He's abused women, supports the Tate brothers and their right to speak hate. His mates would like to see women assigned to a kind of Purdah. He's an outsize playground bully. Not a great surprise that Reform and right wing Conservatives support the guy...'

She sighed and continued.

'...but even this Labour government is cosying up to him instead of standing up to him. That's why they let Gideon escape. They're scared of upsetting Trump and Vance.'

Jonathan nodded.

'But thank you DCI Singh. You've discovered the truth and that is no mean achievement. We'll speak truth unto power even if they deny it or wave their clean hands at us, like Pontius Pilate. We've nothing to lose. But the two of us are not in the right place to do it, at this moment in time. Nasreen and I have no one to leave all this to now. We must decide how best to honour our daughter. One idea is to give scholarships to study in Oxford to young women from countries where female education is not valued.'

Ranjit told them about his football project.

'We'd be delighted to support you. Let us be patrons and pay for the coaching and transport. You'll need to think of a name for the project. Ask some six formers to come up with a logo. They'll know better than our generation what will appeal to teenage boys.'

He showed Ranjit out and pointed to their rose garden.

'Nasreen means 'wild rose' and I planted these for her but I don't know how to please her now.'

***

Jia bought a copy of *The Oxford Mail* on her way home from work and saw the headlines and pictures of Darcy Moss and Gideon Shriver. When Ranjit walked through the door, they wanted to know more. He wasn't keen to talk about the murder. Work of this kind, best not brought home, but they kept pressing him.

'I've just come from the parents. I'd been dreading it especially as they may not get justice for Yasmin. When they talked about honouring her, I found myself telling them about an idea I have and they want to support it. There are good people in the world.'

Amber pointed to the picture of Gideon on the front page.

'It's that creepy guy who sat behind me at Steve Darwin's talk at the Sheldonian. He kept kneeing me in the small of my back and then apologising in a snooty style.'

Ranjit's faced drained. He hugged his daughter and held her tight until she looked embarrassed. That night he and Jia went to bed early. She massaged him to try to relax him. He wanted to make love to her but the need to talk was stronger.

'The thought that that man touched my daughter makes my skin creep. How can I protect her? I want her to feel free but this horror seems to threaten even my family.'

Jia kissed him and said,

'Do you know what they've enjoyed this year? You've watched them play football and taken them out for a meal after matches. That's what they want of their father; his time and love and good humour.'

'There was a brief moment when we interviewed Moss when I almost felt sorry for him. He seemed to believe he was like a father to Gideon. Love and compassion is what all religions teach and yet twisted versions lead to violence, abuse and misery. It turns love into a desire to control. But, Moss? He was trying to love Gideon.'

'Let's go to the Gurdwara on Sunday. It'll help you.'

'You're right. I need you Jia. I don't tell you often enough that I love you. This job isn't good for family life, is it? Shall I rethink? Join the probation service?'

'I'll support whatever you want to do but don't make any rushed decisions in the mood you're in or you'll choose badly. What you need is a holiday. Can you get time off at the summer half term? Let's go to India again and this time to the foothills of the Himalayas. It will ground you in nature.'

Chapter 39

Kate asked Ranjit if they could go for a drink at the end of the week. They chose to meet at the Victoria Arms and take a walk beside the Cherwell.

'We didn't get off to the best start, but, I want to thank you for supporting me when I went behind your back and asked Steve to get his ethical hacker onto Gideon.'

'Without that Kate, Moss wouldn't have confessed – at least not to us. It was on his conscience so, at some point, he'd have confessed to a priest but that wouldn't have got to us so we wouldn't have nailed him or Gideon.

'Life plays strange tricks doesn't it? For twenty years my ambition was to become a DCI. I was not the best husband because I was frustrated, believing it could never happen given the racism in the MET. I uprooted my family to fulfil my dream. This case has made me rethink. Would I be better working in the probation service? Make a difference, change lives?'

'That's a bombshell. You're a damn good DCI and the team respects you. To say we would miss you is an understatement but it's your life and your decision.'

'That means a lot. The reason I'm feeling like this is because central command, the government and secret services saw me as a convenient scapegoat who would take the rap when we failed. The exception was Thomas Said. He at least was collaborative. Despite succeeding against the odds, I doubt we'll receive much in the way of thanks. If you and the team hadn't supported me, I'd have been utterly alone.'

***

Kate hadn't seen Sam since the ordeal at Abingdon Way. They talked about Steve leaving and Kate asked,

'Have you lost much money?

'Steve was such a nice guy. He gave me next month's rent and I can start advertising now. Even if I can't get a booking immediately, there's plenty of demand in June. I panicked when my regulars at the gym cancelled but they've returned: they didn't want their photos on TV. Because of the publicity, I'm getting enquiries and new clients. Some are local but say they didn't know there was a gym in Thames Reach.

'I'm fine but I worry about Alex. She was in shock after finding Yasmin's body. Steve was bringing her to life and hope again. It seemed to me that she was falling for him and now he's gone-just like that.' She clicked her fingers.

George was working in Sam's garden and asked why they looked so concerned.

'It's Alex. She's not working or cooking and that's unlike her. She can't forgive herself for talking to that reporter.'

***

George and Alex sat having coffee in her garden.

'You need a dose of medicine, natural medicine. I've been planning to walk the Ridgeway. Join me. I'd love your company and being away from Thames Reach and in nature will help you put all that's happened into perspective.

'Don't misunderstand me. This is a like-minded friendship, we won't be sharing a room on the way.'

Kate and Sam thought it a brilliant idea.

'George wants to start not far from Tring on Ivinghoe Beacon. I've never been to the museum there. It sounds bizarre with its taxidermy. But everyone I know who's visited it has learned a lot. Ranjit took his twins and said it was the tiger that made the biggest impression on them. Let's all go together and Sam, Goldie and I'll wave you off afterwards,' said Kate to Alex.

Chapter 40

Alex and George had arrived in Oxfordshire to what Alex decided was her favourite spot on the Ridgeway, White Horse Hill with its chalk white carving etched into the treeless green.

'The horse looks contemporary, George, minimalist even – not art created 3,500 years ago.'

'Over there is where you slay your dragons,' said George pointing to Dragon Hill. 'The locals have always associated it with my saintly namesake – George the dragon slayer.'

'Let's walk on it and tackle the enemies of my mind and tell new stories,' smiled Alex.

But first they sat, opened their flask and sipped tea looking down over the village of Uffington.

'This place feels like a time machine. Down there, people are in the present. Up here we're in bed with the past, ancient but alive in the molecules of light. Sorry, George, you must think I'm mad, the way I'm talking.'

'It's a timeless feeling, walking the Ridgeway,' he replied.

'You're right. We've been walking where our ancestors wearing woad walked, worked and...' she paused and looked towards him, 'made love. The path ahead is the future. Do you sense the magic, George?'

'For me that's the magic,' he said pointing to a buzzard flying above them and further away where kites were circling. But I know what you mean. You feel that men and women have walked here for thousands of years. So you're glad you came?'

'Thank you George. It's given me hope and a new purpose.'

Alex's gaze fell on the eye of the horse.

'You and Kate were right about me and history. I've had enough of crime. It's the bestselling genre and I needed to pay the bills but with the TV contract going ahead, I can please myself.

'I'll try historical fiction and the first novel set here? There'll be the dilemmas, the friendships, the love and the hate and violence, but it won't be set *now*. I'll be able to escape into the past. Fact and fiction won't meet in my life.'

Acknowledgements

Readers will realise that Reptiles is up-to-the-minute both locally and internationally. When St Hilda's College bought Radley Large Wood, we thought it was in safe hands. But the destruction, with the resulting sea of mud and loss of habitat, that we witnessed in late 2024 early 2025 led to some of us establishing the Friends of Radley Large Wood. One of the founders, Paul Gamble, happens to have the same surname as a nature-loving character in my novel. As well as being a naturalist, classicist and wildlife photographer, Paul is a poet. He and local crime writer, Steve Lunn, read an early version and gave me sound advice and fantastic feedback as did my well-travelled friend, Haldi Sheahan. Many thanks to the three of them for their invaluable help.

I'd also like to thank Katie Isbester of Claret Press and Clapham Publishing for her continued support. Without her, I would not be a published novelist.
www.claretpress.com and www.claphampublishing.com

Thanks to the talented Petya Tsankova for the cover and design of the book.

I worried about the Iranian aspect of the story, so was delighted when Mark Turner produced
https://www.youtube.com/watch?v=Df5yMsPfCWY

Mark is a fellow member of an informal networking group of journalists, film makers and freelance writers – like me. We meet on the first Tuesday of every month to share a beer. Mark's documentary led to a sigh of relief on my behalf that I had it right.

Thanks to everyone who holds woodland in their hearts. Together I hope that we can safeguard our natural world for the next generation.

What's a book without readers? THANK YOU!

Endorsements of Sylvia's books

Brushstrokes in Time (set in the USA and China)
(Claret Press)

A Brilliant Compelling Read.
Shrenik Rao, Editor of the Madras Courier

Among my top ten historical novels, certainly of this century. Utterly mesmerising and unforgettable.
Dr Jenny Lewis, poet and teacher (Oxford University)

I couldn't put this page-turner down. As I reached the end just one thought dominated: everyone should read this book. No one I've come across has managed to tell the story of modern Chinese politics, arts and society in such accessible, imaginative and compelling a fashion.
Ray Foulk: Founder of the Isle of Wight Festival & author of Stealing Dylan from Woodstock.

Vetta is always accurate with a grasp of vivid detail.
John Gittings: Chief Foreign Correspondent of the Guardian.

Food of Love, cooking up a life across gender, class and race.
(Claret Press)

Told with brio and verve, this is an astonishing life story that takes in working-class life in post-war Britain, and the transformation of society in the decades that followed.
Rana Mitter: Professor of the History and Politics of Modern China, the Universities of Oxford and Harvard.

Food of Love is a testimony of zest for life, and compassionate anger at the many forms of injustice in post-war England. Sylvia Vetta's story takes us through her many lives, as she reinvents herself time and time again, rising from the ashes of prejudice, misogyny, racism and greed to renew herself.
Jane Spiro: Professor of Education and TESOL, Oxford Brookes University

Not So Black and White by Sylvia Vetta
and Nancy Mudenyo Hunt
(Set in London and west Kenya)
(The Nasio Trust)

The Book to read after the Black Lives Matter protests.
The Oxford Times

Timey, pacey and personal novel.
Love Reading

Current of Death: This debut crime novel has a complex and interesting plot, which explores important issues in contemporary life: Mystery People

About the Author

Sylvia is on her third career after teaching and running a business. She was a freelance writer for *The Oxford Times* and various art and antiques magazines for twenty years. The castaway series, which she wrote for ten years in *The Oxford Times,* was turned into three books. Despite that, Sylvia couldn't find an agent so thought her first historical novel , *Brushstrokes in Time,* would stay on her computer. A small but traditional publisher, Claret Press, admired it and published it. It has received seventy 5*reviews on Amazon and been endorsed by China experts, poets, editors and academics.

With Ray Foulk, James Harrison and Andy Severn, she founded the Oxford Indie Book Fair to support small publishers and authors. It takes place in November in the iconic Oxford University Examination Schools. You can meet her there. She's a champion of libraries for upward mobility and for developing a love of reading in children. She co-founded the Friends of Radley Large Wood which appears in this novel.

https://www.sylviavetta.co.uk
https://www.oxfordindiebookfair.co.uk
https://www.facebook.com/sylvia.vetta